"My body was like a battleground, marked with the humiliating signs of defeat. During every fit I got bruised, and bumped, grazed, cut, scratched, jolted, broken, or shaken, according to how I fell, from what height, and against which piece of furniture, or doorknob, banister railing, bed-end, or fire-guard I landed."   —from *Black Water*

"Against the background of Victorian England, evoked in a manner reminiscent of a Dickens novel, Rachel Anderson . . . has constructed the story of an epileptic child who surmounts fearsome odds to achieve a life for himself. A memorable novel which is as much a portrait of an age as it is of an individual."   —*Horn Book*

BLACK WATER

RACHEL ANDERSON

The Putnam & Grosset Group

Library of Congress Cataloging-in-Publication Data
Anderson, Rachel.
Black water / Rachel Anderson.
p.   cm.
Summary: Albert is an epileptic who lives a cloistered life
with his mother in nineteenth-century England, and while she
deludes herself searching for a miracle cure, Albert eventually begins
to accept his condition and to become self-reliant.
[1. Epilepsy—Fiction.   2. Self-acceptance—Fiction.
3. Mothers and sons—Fiction.   4. England—Fiction.]   I. Title.
PZ7.A5489B1   1995   [Fic]—dc20   94-37603
ISBN 0-698-11421-3
1   3   5   7   9   10   8   6   4   2

With thanks to Ann Freeman
for her help

One

On Wednesday we moved to new lodgings, Mother and I. In those days we were always on the move, never able to remain long in any establishment. Sometimes we stayed less than a week. I would have preferred to settle in one place in the way that I supposed ordinary folk settled. These constant moves seemed always to be, in some unspoken way, my fault.

She had taken two rooms for us at a place she said was named Mortlake.

"A bedroom and a parlour. At the front. And very nearly on the first floor. It's really a most pleasant area. I think we'll find it agreeable."

"Mortlake?" I said. It did not seem a very agreeable name for a place that supposed itself to be pleasant.

"It means, my dear, that it is near to a river."

At any rate a river should be of interest, with boats and beachcombing and fishing and maybe other boys I could get to speak to.

"You see, Albert dear, people of distinction always like to live by a rive. The sight of moving water is calming to the soul. Furthermore, Mortlake is close by a fashionable area."

How, I wondered, could a place named after death become fashionable, unless those fashionable people were necrophiles?

"*Mort* only means 'death' when it is in French, dear. In English it loses that meaning. When you come to learn French, you will find there are many words like that. They seem one thing, but they are quite another."

Since I had no other teachers, I had to believe what she told me.

"Mortlake, as you will find, although not actually *in* royal Richmond, is on the periphery. And Richmond is said to be very pleasant indeed. There is a spacious park which has belonged to royalty through aeons of time. Her majesty's own royal deer roam there freely, so I have heard. I believe they are red, which is, of course, a royal hue." She smiled to herself at the thought.

Mother was interested in all aspects of royalty, who they married, what they wore, where they built houses, and now even in the colour of their animals.

"And we'll be conveniently close by Sheen, too. Another exceedingly nice neighbourhood. It means 'the shining place.' Isn't that a lovely thing to say? There'll be some pleasant people there, too. I have no doubt."

Mother was a teacher of flower drawing, pianoforte, a little singing, and some French. While the social standing of any future neighbours was of no personal concern to me, it was in my interest to live near to pleasant people, for they were more likely than unpleasant ones to require that their

4

daughters acquired a certain skill at dainty drawing, foreign conversation-making, and playing simple tunes on the piano.

When we arrived in Mortlake, I could see no river. One would hardly have known, apart from the strange dank smell in the air and a sea gull overhead, that there was any river, such was the huddle and muddle and higgle-piggle of buildings and warehouses. The carrier set us down at the end of Water Lane, a cobbled dead-end so narrow it was quite in shadow.

We had to carry our own luggage to the lodging-house steps.

The keeper grudgingly agreed to lift our things inside, and Mother proceeded grandly up the wooden stairs more as though she had booked into a first-floor suite at the Victoria Royal in Bath.

The walls of the stairwell were patchy and discoloured. The stairs were uncarpeted. Through a window on the half-way landing I caught a glimpse of the fashionable river, so wide and flat that it seemed scarcely to move, its still surface grey and greasy.

The peculiar smell of the area, as I later came to learn, was due to the density of manufacturing businesses hugging the river's edge to benefit from the flowing water to remove their waste products. The brewery issued a thick cloying smell of fermenting yeast into the air and a foaming turgid liquid into the water. There was, too, a carpet works and a candle-maker's as well as a storage place for hemp and rope, produced further upstream and awaiting transportation down to London.

The warehouses backed directly on to the river so that,

short of entering a property through the front and jumping from a window at the back, there was no way a person could actually reach the water for the boyish pleasure of boating or fishing or splashing about as I had romantically envisaged.

We reached the second floor.

"There now! And what do you think of that, then?" said Mother as she unlocked and flung open the door of our new quarters. "Rather better than the usual, wouldn't you say?"

These were not first-floor rooms, but at any rate not third or fourth floor, nor lower ground. We had been in some airless attics, and some dark humid basements, in our time.

Our parlour had heavy plum curtains and, before an empty grate, a blue ottoman on which I would doubtless have to sleep. These were not really two rooms but one large room with a recess hidden behind a dividing curtain hanging on brass rings. I could tell already that the horsehair stuffing of the ottoman's upholstery was hard and lumpy and dusty. The high mahogany bed in the recess, where Mother would sleep, would be little better.

Yet she seemed more than satisfied with our latest home.

"What a pleasant view we have from here," she said, removing her hatpins and her hat.

There was no view, apart from blank brick walls and warehouse windows.

"Look, I do believe we can see almost to the river. That spur of pretty green, that'll be the willows growing on the banks. Bending gracefully to embrace the water. At least, I think that'll be river-willows. Over to the left. Do you see?"

There was a blur between the close-packed buildings

which might have been the low-hanging foliage of a tree, and might equally have been a pile of decaying refuse tinted with the green of algae.

"Yes, Mother." I tried to see what she wished me to see.

We were of necessity close. I didn't know if it was normal to be so confined to one another's company. We were more like two whelks cowering inside the same shell than a parent and her son. But as I so rarely mingled with others I knew little of what was done in normal society.

"There's just us two in the world," she sometimes told me. "You must love me and do what I say and I'll take care of you, whatever anybody else says."

"Yes, Mother."

Why, I wondered, did she say these rooms were better than usual when they appeared to be dingier and less well furnished than the last place? Why did she turn everything back to front, deny what was true, and make false claims?

It was all very vexing.

I looked at the soot and dingy pigeon feathers heaped in the empty grate. I said, "I hope there are no rats."

At a previous lodging there had been an infestation of rats in our basement and bugs in the beds.

"Here," she said, "there are definitely no vermin."

When I was younger I trusted her utterly. She told me everything there was to know of the world, or so I believed. And I, in return, revealed everything that was on my mind.

Because we were so enclosed, I had no one but her to tell of the dark oppressive cliffs and the shivering splintering star-lights that sometimes assaulted me. She dismissed these confessions as insignificant.

"You're a funny chap," she would say, tousling my hair.

"What fanciful ways you have. Such pretty visions and make-up dreams you keep in that little old head of yours."

They were not dreams. I was not making them up. They were not pretty.

"But I was so afraid, Mother," I said. "It seemed so real. I thought I was falling into pieces."

Of late, when I confided in her, she was not inclined to listen.

"Don't go on about it, there's a good chap."

"No, Mother. I'm sorry." I didn't want her to be angry with me when she was the only person I had in the world.

"If you don't dwell on them, these silly things will pass. You will grow out of them."

I was not growing out of them. Rather, I was beginning to grow out of the single cramped shell we shared. Things had begun imperceptibly to change between us.

Meanwhile, the episodes, for I knew no other word to describe them, had begun to take on a new dimension.

Hitherto, they caused no pain. I was scarcely aware that they had occurred. I crossed the room, yet did not know *how* I had crossed it. The sequence of consciousness was so little broken by the episode that, after it had happened, it seemed that hardly an atom of time was missing. I knew that they had occurred only by the numb sensation in the centre of the brain.

Increasingly, the experience lasted longer and with a greater ferocity. I seemed to disappear from the world and return much later, without knowing where I had been.

"Mother, sometimes I get afraid. What is it that happens when the world disappears? Where do I go to? Where do *you* go? Why don't you come with me? I feel I am disintegrating, that I'm dying."

She looked away and plucked with irritation at the plush curtains. She did not offer comfort.

"Mother, do you think that I am dead when I go away?"

She turned on me angrily and hissed in a low whisper. "Shh! I don't ever wish to hear you speak about these things. You will only make it worse for both of us if you talk like that. Anybody might be listening. What if the wind changed while you were saying it? Then you'd be stuck with it forever."

The lodging-house keeper came grumbling up the stairs with our luggage, assisted by a tall youth. We had a tin trunk containing Mother's music, her cartridge papers, and her watercolour paints, and two pigskin bags with solid brass hinges and someone's initials engraved on the locks.

The man dumped her tin trunks on the carpet and Mother quickly resumed her air of busy optimism.

"Come along now, my dear. Don't just stand there like a post. We must quickly get ourselves unpacked and sorted out."

The boy carried in our two leather bags.

We had acquired them, if I understood Mother right, from a fellow resident at one of the boardinghouses we'd stayed in. He had been unexpectedly arrested early one morning, leaving all his possessions behind.

He had, so Mother said, called out to us through the barred window of the Black Maria, which took him away, "Dear madam, it's room fourteen. Please help yourself to whatever you fancy." So she had taken the pigskin bags.

"A useful thing worth knowing, dear. To create a good impression, it always pays to have good-looking luggage. You never know who might be watching your arrival. One can tell a good deal about a person by the quality of their cases."

The initials of the detained person in the back of the Black Maria were B.H.F., but I never found out what his name had been. Perhaps he had been an actor or travelling showman, for inside one of the bags had been a book containing tales based on the plays by William Shakespeare. I read every one of them before we mislaid the book during one of our moves.

The old man shuffled out but the youth hung hopefully in the doorway. Mother fetched her purse and opened it slowly and deliberately as though unsure what creature might be lurking inside ready to leap out.

The boy watched her with bulging lustrous eyes. His head and feet were inordinately large, his feet almost horse-like, while his arms hung at his sides, long and skinny, and there was a strange animal odour about him. However, he had a nice enough expression. Perhaps if we stayed here long enough I might get to speak with him. But he was so far beneath my own station I would have to approach him only when Mother was out at a pupil's home.

"And another thing well worth the knowing," said Mother, "and that is tipping. If you wish to go up in the world, it pays dividends to tip with confidence. At any rate at the beginning. Especially in a place like this, which has had connections with royalty since the days of Henry the Fourth."

I did not wish to go up in the world. I did not wish to go anywhere. I wanted us to stay still in one place for long enough to find out what happened to me each time the world stopped still and I disappeared.

Mother graciously handed the boy a ha'penny as though it were half a guinea, then said grandly, "We wish our dinner brought up at four o'clock."

He blinked, which was as though he had said, Yes.

He was only a simple boot-boy but seemed happy enough to oblige her by acting like a footman.

"And what do we have on the menu for today?"

"Mutton. Boiled."

"Very well. That will be all for now."

She looked happy to have moved so near to her dream paradise, the green pastures of right royal Richmond where the red deer roamed.

In the afternoon, Mother had a singing pupil to visit. I unbuckled the leather strap from her tin trunk, and Mother selected some drawing-room ballads to take to her pupil. "Child of the Flowing Tide," "Come Into the Garden, Maud," and "The Swans Swim So Bonny" were silly maudlin songs and I told her so. Mother muttered under her breath that since Miss Barker sang like a donkey it hardly mattered what words issued from her mouth.

Mother fetched her bonnet and gloves. She would be taking the omnibus as far as Tollcross, changing to a cab for the last few hundred yards so that, should anyone at the Barkers' be watching out, she would be seen arriving in a suitable manner for a pleasant teacher of pleasant young ladies.

Suddenly, on a whim, I did not want to be left behind, alone in this grubby room.

"Mother, I must come with you."

"Of course you can't," she said, alarmed.

"Why not?"

"Because the high road is noisy and dangerous. You might get hurt."

"But *you* are going there. The risk for you is just as great."

"It is too noisy for you."

"I don't mind. I have nothing to do here."

"You have the hollyhocks."

"Why do you never let me come, too?"

"Because it just wouldn't do. I dare say you'll understand when you're older."

"But I want to see Miss Barker, even if she does sing like a donkey."

"I never said that!" said Mother. "I mentioned merely that Miss Barker's singing is still at an excessively elementary level."

"You did! You did! Definitely a donkey."

"Then I am shocked at my own indiscretion."

"And since she sings like a donkey, there's every reason for me to want to come and see if she looks like one, too. Though with her name, it might be better if she sang like a dog. Or else changed her name to Bray."

Mother told me to watch my tongue lest it ran away with me and led us both into deep water. "And then where would we be?"

I did not succeed in making her change her mind.

In whatever place we lived, Mother always ensured that the door to our room was furnished with a mortice lock and supplied with two keys, one for her, one for me. Where there was no lock, she would call up a locksmith to make the necessary adjustment.

As she left for Miss Barker, she checked that all was well.

"Albert, do you have the key?"

"Yes, Mother."

She would not take my word that the key was in my pocket. I had to show it.

"Then as soon as I am gone, you secure the door behind me. And remove your key from the lock."

"Yes, Mother. Of course."

"Once I have gone, you will sit here quietly at the table and get on with your task."

She had laid out for me the tiny palettes of paint, the set of fine brushes, the old cockleshells on which we mixed the colours, the little rags we used for wiping the sable brush tips, the other rag for wiping the pen-nibs, the papers, and the rough picture of the hollyhock that was the guide. Mother had been selling flower designs to a printer of fancy artwork who used them for greeting cards, folding fans, hanging calendars, and other paper novelties.

Recently Mother had been teaching me to copy-paint the flowers. Each one took many hours of detailed painstaking work. It kept me occupied when she was away. When it became apparent that I had some considerable talent for it, she had taken to submitting my copies to the printer in lieu of her own. Naturally she said nothing about not having done them herself for fear that if they were known to be from the hand of a mere boy, less money would be forthcoming. "Yes, Mother. Of course."

"And you'll make sure you get the blossoms the right size so they are quite clearly hollyhocks, and not lupins or delphiniums?"

"Yes, Mother."

"And not move till I return."

She had no need to fuss. My copy painting was already more accurate than her own and my sense of colour more subtle. I was interested in making each picture seem as realistic as possible. I was proud, too, to be making this small but not insignificant contribution to our income.

"And if you feel poorly, you must keep as quiet as you can. Now that you are old enough, it is up to you to keep utterly silent and no one need know."

"But when must I keep quiet, Mother?" I asked.

"Shhh."

I suspected that whatever it was that must be kept so secret was connected in some way with my disappearances. But how would I find out what happened then if I was not there to see and if she would not speak about it?

Other grown children, I noticed, did not stay indoors. From upper windows I looked down and saw them, bowling hoops along the street, playing in backyards. I was coming to discover that in some way which I had yet to learn I was not like other children.

"Now lock the door behind me."

When I had done so, she tried the handle from the outside to make sure. Then she called softly through the keyhole. "Albert? Have you taken out your key?"

"Yes, Mother." I tapped it on the door panelling so she would be reassured.

"Very well, dear."

I heard her departing footsteps tip-tapping away down the wooden stairs, leaving me a prisoner. Yet since I had a key I was in voluntary captivity, imprisoned by my own hand and apparently for my own good.

She would be returning for our dinner at four o'clock. So

I had enough time to get a good start on the flowers. But first I had to make a thorough examination of our room so that I might come to own the details and feel that it was indeed home.

On the walls was faded paper and on the floor a piece of faded carpet.

I detected a strange organic smell rising from the floor. When I bent to identify it, I sensed it was coming, not from the carpet, but up through the floorboards from some room below. It must be the mutton for our dinner, a poor old ewe simmering in a lake of grease, her trotters dancing, toes up, amongst the swimming scallions.

The pattern on the faded walls was of strange birds with elongated tails on a paisley background. The birds began languidly to flap their wings and flex their tails.

The blue paisley lozenges behind them began to float.

I recognized them. I had seen them before. I had been here in this room with these floating lozenges and flapping birds at this precise moment before. But how was that possible when we had moved to Mortlake only that day?

Something strange was about to happen. Music was tumbling through the air. The heavenly host was coming down here into this earthly room. But when I listened, the singing changed in pitch to chanting, then to screaming. No longer angels but imps of Satan. Then it was the wailing of perished souls in purgatory, or the bleet of a weeping sheep. Their tremendous noise built up in my ears to a colossal pitch like a bell ringing, but not a bell. It was ringing at the wrong pitch for an ordinary bell.

The strange odour seeped upwards through the cracks in the floor, now so nauseous that I felt it would suffocate me.

The floor heaved like a great rolling sea-wave. The walls bulged as though their membranes would burst and all the liquid inside would come leaking out.

Disgust rose out of the fabric of that rotting waterside building, engulfing me, smothering me in a vapour.

"You have to let me out, let me out of here!" I cried but the wrong sounds came from my throat. I staggered to the door and hammered with my fist.

"Mama, Mama, save me. Let me out. Open the door for me."

But my tongue would not obey my thoughts.

Then I saw how curiously the doorknob began to turn by itself, to left and right, and simultaneously I tasted the steely taste of metal in my mouth as though I had licked the metal with my tongue, which could open doors but could not speak words.

The bird-patterned walls were breathing. The glass droplets on the lampshade trembled with a shrill tinkle.

I had to get away. We all had to get away. I ran to the window. But the light piercing through the pane was too bright.

I heard voices outside the door. Mother would save me. She promised to take care of me. Her voice was calling to me through the keyhole.

I fumbled with the key in the lock and flung open the door just in time. The boot-boy stood there with an empty ash bucket held in his long thin arms.

He spoke. I watched the wide mouth open and close like a pike drowning in an excess of air. I heard no sound.

I opened my own mouth to warn him. But before any words could be formed, a roaring as of water crashing over a precipice filled the air.

"Blimey, laddie, you all right?" he said.

I raised my hand to point to the bulging walls of the landing, to the heaving staircase. But it was too late for any of us. We had to succumb to the inevitable.

"What, you got sunstroke or something?"

Those were the last words before the darkness.

And then nothing and nothing.

Two

———❧———

S omething had occurred which was, I feared, of some immense significance. But my mind was so befuddled that I could not fathom what. I knew only that it must have been a catastrophe on a national, or even international, scale, affecting thousands of the population in the same way that it had affected me.

Perhaps a volcano?

I slid down from the high bed and crept cautiously across to the casement. The joints of my body ached. Its limbs were uncoordinated, moving like a marionette with slackened strings. I drew back the heavy curtains, folded back the shutters, let up the blind and looked out.

No, it had not been a volcano, for there was no lava flooding down the narrow lane, as had happened at Pompeii according to an interesting engraving I had seen in *The Illustrated London News*, nor asphyxiating dust clogging my lungs.

Then an earthquake?

No, for the ground would have cracked open, the river

overflowed its banks, many buildings would have been destroyed with much loss of life. This, too, I had read about in the interesting *Illustrated London News*. The buildings around me were still intact. There were no bodies strewn on the lane outside, except for that of a sleeping dog and a drunk woman, back to back, in the gutter. Besides, Mortlake was said to be close by a fashionable town, not known for its earthquakes any more than for its volcanoes.

I wished, not for the first time, that I attended school so that my knowledge of natural disasters might be more extensive. I had to rely on Mother's tuition, and the source of her information came, like mine, almost entirely from back issues of *The Illustrated London News*. Their discussion of volcanoes and earthquakes had been dramatically entertaining rather than enlightening.

The event must have been on a more mundane scale, perhaps a storm in which I had been struck by lightning.

Certainly, I recalled the violent light piercing through the windowpane, though it must have been a rainless storm. The surface of Water Lane below me was dry.

My head throbbed. I wondered if I had taken a fever. Yet I was neither too hot nor too cold, although I felt exceedingly weak.

I was mistaken in assuming it to have been an event affecting the physical world when it had been something spiritual and unearthly, a tearing open of the heavens as on the great day of judgement, when strong men shall bow themselves, as it says in the Bible, and the grinders shall cease because they are few.

I groped my way back to the bed. In passing Mother's vanity-glass I caught a glimpse of two swollen eyes coloured purple and yellow like the little heart's-ease flower with its gold and violet face. I hauled myself up onto the bed and saw how the bolster-slip was smeared with the red that fades to the brownish colour of bracken as it dries. I licked my cracked lips and tasted that familiar metallic taste. Had I been attacked by thieves?

I lay back and rested.

At four o'clock, there was a light scraping at the door. It was the boot-boy thumping with his foot. He shuffled in with a dinner tray which he set down beside me on the bed-cover.

How odd that Mother was not yet back.

"Excuse me," I said, "but did you notice anything strange about today?"

He gave me a slow stare with wet cowlike eyes but said nothing. His long thin arms hung by his sides.

"Has there been a thunderstorm? Or artillery?"

He shrugged his shoulders and pointed with his fist to the covered dish on the tray. He made eating movements with his jaw and then gestured to me to look at the tray. Was this a deaf-mute?

I lifted the cover of the dish.

The meat was pale grey and smelt of fish.

"Fish?" I said. "I thought it was going to be mutton."

He was not dumb or deaf. He nodded. "Fish. Always get fish Fridays."

He went out, letting the door slam behind him. It rattled inside my skull as though my brains were twisted.

I was not hungry for fish any more than I had been hungry for mutton. And I did not understand why it should be fish when, earlier, the boy had surely promised us mutton.

Why did he say there was always fish on Friday when it was Wednesday? Wednesday was most certainly the day we moved here from our previous lodging.

I went after him. He was halfway down the stairwell, clomping heavily with his horselike feet. I called. "Excuse me again, please, but what day is it today?"

He hesitated, then continued on his way.

I said, "Did you say Friday?"

He nodded, then paused and turned. "I have work to do. I cannot pass the time of day with you. But don't take offence."

Despite his uncouth appearance, he seemed almost apologetic.

"Oh. Very well, I see."

No doubt the swollen eyes, coloured like wild pansies, and the blood-smeared night-shirt were unsettling to a servant boy.

"I'm sorry," I said. "I won't bother you anymore."

If today truly was Friday, then I had mislaid two days. How could they go so easily? Before, when I had disappeared, I returned almost immediately. How could time disappear in on itself? Perhaps it had been eaten away as rotten flesh is eaten away by mould and decay? Perhaps it had been stolen by the devil to use for his own devices in the same way that young children are stolen?

As I retreated, the servant turned and came back up the stairs after me.

"Listen, laddie," he whispered, "you been concussed. Knocked out. Stone cold like a fist-fighter."

"Who hit me?"

"No one hit you. You done it to yourself."

Self-mutilation?

"Shouldn't be telling you. I'll cop it if Giddings finds me out. But since you've got an agreeable face . . ."

How remarkable of him to say the same thing of me that I had earlier thought of him—that he had an amiable face. How doubly strange of him when my face was at that moment far from pleasing.

"And you seem a good enough little laddie, so I may as well let you in on what they said."

He leant over the bannisters to check that no one was on the lower landing, then indicated silently by hand gestures that he wanted to follow me back into the room. He closed the door behind us.

He said, "And that's not the half of it. The verdict is, you're a loony."

"A loony?" I didn't understand. Perhaps it was some uncouth slang, some term of abuse popular with common folk.

"You know, cracked, upper storey to let, not all there."

"Am I?"

"Not common barmy. Something a bit more special, from what I understood. They called the physician in. They was going to fetch a constable, too, when you were raving. There was that much noise they thought you were some unholy drunk till they got up here and saw you was just a poor little mite. Old Giddings reckons you should be put away."

"Put away? Where would that be?"

"One of them new asylums, you know, for lunatics."

I knew the meaning of the word lunatic well enough. I said, "You mean, I am demented?"

"Could say."

I clutched at the curtain to support me.

"And right now I reckon you look like you ought to get in that bed."

He helped me back.

"And eat up your nice dinner. Fish is good for the brains and that's what you're needing."

But I wasn't hungry for fish any more than I might have been hungry for swimming mutton.

"I'll wait to eat till my mother is back," I said.

"She's out, won't be back till eight. It'll be stone cold by then."

He gazed down at the grey fish growing clammy on the dish with a look in his big wet eyes that was not disgust but yearning.

"You have it then," I said, pushing the tray to him. "If you really want it."

"You sure? Just so long as this dementia you got isn't infectious."

"How should I know?"

He knelt down by the bed as though to begin his evening prayers and swiftly gobbled everything on the plate, the flesh, the skin, the watery juice, the seeping potatoes.

I asked, "Don't you get any dinner?"

He nodded. "Of course. But it's my destiny to be hungry, just like it's yours to be mad. Maybe I got an unpaying visitor lodging with me."

I didn't know what he meant.

"You don't know much. Think I got a little tapeworm living with me, lodging in my insides, eating up what by rights is mine."

When the plate was licked clean, he inspected Mother's paints set out on the table.

"You just know about them pretty flowers, you do. Funny thing for a boy." Then he noticed my compendium of games on the mantelshelf, in a plain wooden box, inlaid with patterns made from coloured foreign timber from trees in faraway lands. He lifted it down from the shelf with a slow grin and slid open the lid. The box contained the pieces and boards to play dominoes, ludo, and chess. Chinese chequers, Nine Men's Morris, and halma. He looked at the pieces curiously as though he had no idea what they were for. He was wretchedly ignorant. He picked out a domino piece and stared at it.

"It's black," he said. "With white dots."

"It's a domino. For a game. Do you want to play?"

I set out the pieces on the back of the dinner tray. He took a long time to master the rules. Although I tried my best not to win, sadly I beat him seven times out of seven. He was not in the least put out.

"You're not half a bright player for a bedlamite boy!" he said with admiration.

I suggested we play a different game, but I had no success at teaching him some rudimentary chess moves. However, we did better with ludo but nobody was the winner because we heard the lodging-house keeper hollering out in the yard and had to abandon the game before either of us got any of our counters to Home.

As he was leaving with the dinner tray, the boy asked, "Is it all right then, being loony? You look like you're none too bothered by it."

I could have explained that, in all honesty, I did not yet know how it felt as I was still getting accustomed to the state.

"You should eat more food," he said. "It's not good to go hungry. I'll fetch you up some broth when Giddings isn't about."

As soon as he had gone, I found the small red-hide diary which Mother had given me last Christmastime. I took one of the drawing pens from the table, unscrewed the cap of the Indian ink, dipped in the steel nib, and in the diary marked a black cross against Wednesday. That was the day of the episode. When it happened again, as it surely would, I would be better prepared. I would mark another cross. If I was to be mad, I had to have some way of keeping an account of days lost to me.

When Mother returned, she did not respond to my greeting with her usual peck on the cheek. Perhaps she found the battered face too offensive. Instead, she busied about tidying and dusting with her pocket handkerchief, with scarcely a glance at me.

Inside the bruised skull, her scurryings and ratlike scratchings took on the volume of rodent cannon-charges. They were increasingly difficult to bear. The head pain, which had been temporarily relieved while the boot-boy was with me, had renewed its bite.

Mother did not refer to my madness. Indeed, she made no mention of the fact that I was lying in her bed in a stained night-shirt with two swollen eyes, nor did she refer to the obliteration of two days of life.

Now that I knew my problem was insanity, I, too, said nothing about anything.

At least I understood now why she would not take me

when she went to her pupils' homes. With a bedlamite boy in tow, she would lose them all. But how, I wondered, would they *know* that I was mad? Could a person tell just by observing? Was my face so different? Were my limbs different from other boys'?

I felt my left arm along its length, from the upper arm, to the knobbly elbow, down the fleshy forearm, then the flexible wrist and the strong hand that held a paintbrush or pens, the hand that painted flowers, and along to its finger-tips. Did other boys' hands feel like this or was this hand as mad as its owner?

Of course she could not be humiliated by taking me with her. If I was mad, then so was every part of my being. The boot-boy, with his bulging forehead, his bulbous eyes, and his skinny arms like string, was not mad. I was.

I watched from the pillow as she hung a linen Duchesse-cloth across the frame of the looking-glass to obscure the reflection. I thought its purpose was to soften the light in an already gloomy room. It was not.

"There'll be no need to go peeking at yourself in there, will there, dear?" she said briskly. "No need to brood on the past."

I said, "Will we have to move lodgings again?"

"I dare say."

"*Will* we?"

I should be sad to lose so soon my acquaintance with the boot-boy, the first friendship I had ever struck.

"I shouldn't wonder."

I remained in bed for the remainder of that day and on the one following. At night, Mother slept on the uncomfortable ottoman.

On the third day, Mother considered me to have recovered sufficiently to get up and be taken out for air.

A chance event, witnessed on the towpath of the fashionable river, entirely altered my perception of my madness.

Three

On Sunday Mother took no pupils, for on that day she had the needs of the Almighty to consider. We spent two hours in the parish church with other solemn worshippers, praising the Lord and giving Him thanks for all the many bounteous blessings which He had let flow upon us.

As we knelt in prayer, Mother whispered in my ear, "Don't forget, Albert, to give especial thanks to Him for your very fortunate salvation."

When we emerged from that dark and chilly place, our knees stiff and our eyes blinking in the glare of the outer world, the pleasant people of the congregation conversed sociably, inviting one another to whist parties. Unfortunately we were outsiders to their chatty circle. None spoke to us. It was as though we were invisible. Or perhaps, I suddenly realized, they could see the madness on me as clear as day.

Mother, undaunted by the unfriendliness of pleasant people, said in an unnaturally high voice, "Come now, Albert. We must not be late for our jaunt."

I wondered what she meant. We rarely went on any kind of pleasure outing.

"Yes, a jolly jaunt. You need the colour put back in your cheeks before we go to take the waters at Bath."

This was a lie. We were never going to Bath. Around my bruised eyes I still had plenty of colour. Mother pulled my cap well down on my brow so that the peak hid my eyes from the public gaze.

She was wearing a smart spring bonnet and a new pair of purple kid gloves which I had not seen before that morning. I had presumed that these bright accessories were for the delight of the Almighty, to bring colour into His twilight house.

I was wrong. Mother's sprightly getup was for the benefit of herself and other revellers heading for the refreshment of moving waters.

"Upriver, Albert, to tread where English kings and queens have trod, to frolic where they have frolicked."

We did not travel, as I had hoped, by boat. The only craft that stopped regularly at Mortlake were the big barges. Mother said it was perfectly proper, and also practicable, to use the railway. But arriving at the Richmond railway station, we discovered it was still some distance to the waterfront. However, her instinct for royalty guided her faultlessly through the streets and across an open expanse of grass.

"Look, Albert! The historic Green! What a thrill to stand on the very spot where royalty desported themselves in days of old!"

We saw two dogs desporting themselves and one baby being pushed in a perambulator.

We crossed the Green, which thrilled Mother so greatly, and she located a narrow way named Old Palace Lane. At the end of it we reached a fine mansion right on the water's edge which, unlike the palace, was still intact. But Mother saw no interest in it.

"Built by a minor duke, so insignificant his name is not worthy of recall," she said, hurrying us along to get a glimpse of the property of a far finer duke further up the river.

"The best pleasure-gardens in all the country, with arbours and grottoes, and terraced right down the side of Richmond Hill like the hanging gardens of Babylon, I do believe. We should catch our glimpse from the towpath. The home of the dukes of Buccleuch for simply ever and ever. And what an aspect they must have from their gazebo."

We reached the bridge at Richmond. The white stone gleamed like ivory and the five arches cast their perfectly formed reflections onto the water flowing through.

"That's a good bridge, Mother," I said.

She had to agree that it was, despite the fact that no duke or duchess or king or queen had had anything to do with its construction.

Down on the water there were rowboats and skiffs, and pontoons and pleasure boats, with pleasure-seekers paddling and wading, canoeing and cruising. Above, ambling across the bridge or sauntering at leisure along the towpath, were yet more frolickers, men, women, children, and dogs, also out to enjoy themselves, many dressed in their brightest and gaudiest so that Mother's pink bonnet and mauve gloves no longer seemed out of place.

The air was alive with laughter and merriment and a festival atmosphere, though there was nothing much to do except for the merry people on dry land to watch the cheery people on the water, and vice versa. Never had I been in such a cheerfully populous place.

No one jeered at me for being mad.

Two boys with a hoop came clattering down the path behind us. As they overtook us, one of them tipped off my cap with his stick, tossed it in the air like a pancake, then threw it back for me to catch. Suddenly, I no longer cared who saw the bruising round my eyes. I folded up my cap and shoved it in my pocket.

I, too, could be a pleasure-seeker like the rest. From their carefree manner, these frolickers appeared not to be the pleasant people whose cold company Mother wished to seek, but perfectly ordinary folk, not unlike ourselves.

"Common *hoi polloi*, most of them," she agreed. "From the sound of them. Whitechapel I shouldn't wonder, day-trippers, only here to gawp."

"Isn't that what we're here for?"

"We are here to marvel at history."

I wanted us to be like these other happy people.

Whoever they were, their mood was infectious. Even Mother broke off her discourse on the summerhouse built by King George for his mistress, the Countess of Suffolk, to watch as a paddle-steamer, laden with passengers, and hung with colourful awnings flapping in the breeze, came sturdily through the water towards us. Two ducks skimmed gracefully overhead, and three more bobbed in the wavelets in the wake of the boat. As it drew over to the landing-stage, the crewman jumped off and deftly tied a rope to the mooring-post.

A stream of passengers disembarked to join the crowd ashore. Others rushed excitedly forward to board.

Mother grabbed my hand in her purple gloved one and hurried me to the landing-stage.

"Come, quickly. We'll go, too!"

"Where to?"

"To wherever."

We took seats on deck with an open view to either side, and the steamer proceeded at a stately pace upriver between the green overhanging trees, past the weirs, the houseboats moored in quiet creeks, the tiny sandbank islands, while above the surface, dragonflies with rainbow wings demonstrated the miracle of flight. It was hard to believe that this was the same river as the wide lake that slithered so sluggishly past the warehouses at the end of Water Lane, that these sparkling whirlpools contained the same drops of water as the greasy flow at Mortlake.

We passed thickets of wildflowers and dense green foliage so thick that it screened any hope of a peer at the aristocratic residences which Mother assured me were built all along the way.

Edward the Second, Henry the Sixth, and the Seventh, Catherine of Aragon, Edward the Third, King John, all had their connections with this waterway, and a good many of them, or their children or wives or mistresses or enemies, seemed to have met their life's end in some awesome way hereabouts.

Some children on board were fishing, or attempting to fish, for minnows over the sides, with lengths of string and bent wire. I longed to join them. But Mother insisted I must stay on the bench beside her. In view of my madness, I obeyed.

The boat, it transpired, was going as far as Hampton Court Palace, masterpiece of Henry the Eighth.

"Ah, the panoply of kings," Mother murmured with delight. "What a shame we shan't get as far as Windsor today. Her dear, dear majesty. Such sadness, such fortitude."

Queen Victoria was more often in my mother's thoughts than the Almighty, who bestowed so many blessings upon us. In fact, this queen of ours was as invisible to us as the Almighty, having retired from society into her castle, ever since her husband had died there.

"Poor gracious lady. So young to be left alone in the world."

Mother, too, had been left alone. She, too, was young enough. Yet she did not weep for herself. She had named me after the queen's husband, Prince Albert, as a gesture of loyalty.

When our pleasure craft reached its destination, we disembarked with the crowds right before the main entrance to the huge palace of Hampton Court. It looked nearly as big as the brewery at Mortlake, and Mother went into raptures over the brickwork of the royal walls and the artistry of the royal stone lions on top of the walls.

On the towpath was a great concourse of activity with various ambulant salesmen offering all manner of refreshing things to eat and drink. Several of our fellow passengers, spurning the water-ices and lime soda drinks, hurried off in search of a public house.

"So long as you keep close by me, Albert, then you'll be all right."

If only it had been that simple. If only, by merely keeping close to one's keeper guardian, everything could be all right for a child who had madness.

The fisherboys went to see if they would have better luck casting their lines from the bank than they had from the side of the steamer. Their activity attracted a flotilla of white swans.

"All the swans belong to her majesty!" Mother cried. "Yes, they do, they do!" And she hurried down the bank to admire them as if they themselves were royalty.

I watched her bend forward with her hand stretched out as though to feed them. The sun's bright reflection dazzled on the water beyond her. And at that moment, a perfect Sunday by the water came to an abrupt ending.

Immediately behind me, in the jostle of day-trippers, there was a commotion. I turned as a young woman seemed to be urgently trying to attract my attention.

She staggered a few steps towards me with her mouth moving as if she would speak urgently to me, though there was a blank expression on her face. Her eyes were open and staring. She made several birdlike cries which seemed to be a further attempt to talk. Then she fell to the ground as rigid and stiff as a tree whose trunk has been cut through by an axe. She made no attempt to save herself as she fell.

I stood transfixed, as if rooted to the ground like a neighbouring tree in the same forest.

At my feet, the stiff woman lay, and there followed powerful muscular contractions which swept through her body with such strength that they were squeezing the air from her lungs up through her throat so that she began uttering strange gasping grunts. Her teeth were tightly clenched like a barred gate.

I had never seen any performance like this before. I was horrified, yet could not tear myself away.

"It's a disgusting sight. They shouldn't allow this sort of thing in public," said a passerby, shielding her child's face with her hand so that it could not witness the spectacle, yet enabling the mother herself to watch. "Innocent children should not be obliged to see such things."

"She with you, is she?" another bystander asked me.

I shook my head vehemently. Why should he believe that I was party to this creature's antics?

"They shouldn't be letting people like that out."

"She's drunk."

Two men started to move her.

"Don't touch her!" cried another. "If it's a seizure she'll swallow her tongue. She'll suffocate." He seized a short stick from the ground and began to force it into the young woman's mouth between her parted lips and her closed teeth. But her spasms were too strong to allow this foreign object to gain admittance.

Quite a crowd had gathered, some to enjoy a good view, others to try to save the woman by rushing at her, pulling at her clothes to loosen them. But all movement in the body had ceased and she appeared to be dead. Her complexion lost its colour, turning a dark bluish colour, especially about her lips and above her mouth.

Then, just when it seemed that she might never move again and that any last breath of life was indeed spent, there were respiratory movements visible in an imperceptible rise and fall of her breast.

I watched to see the drama out. No one else's fascination at the horrid spectacle before us could have been as intense as my own. While they watched as disinterested onlookers seeking merely a light distraction on a sunny Sunday outing, I knew without a doubt that I was witnessing a demonstration of my own terrible antics in those times when, as a mad person, I went away. I was filled with revulsion at seeing myself as others must have seen me.

Next, a trickle of clear liquid began to leak out from beneath the woman's rumpled clothing. The trickle became a flow till she was lying in a pool of water. It was her own water. All unaware, she had lost bodily control and urinated in this public place, in full view of all these people. The pool overflowed and created a tiny stream which wandered across the path to the river.

The woman's companion arrived, having procured a cab which waited on the high road. The woman, now partially conscious, was supported to it and borne away. And the following day, as I knew only too well, she would wake in confusion with aching joints and a grinding head pain.

I turned away with tears tickling my eyes and bile rising in my throat.

The crowd began dispersing to find new entertainments. Mother came pushing through the throng, searching for me.

"Albert! Where were you? Come here at once. Come away."

She grabbed my hand and held it hard, not saying a word. Her face was set as she hurried me towards the landing-stage. She seemed very angry.

Four

‹‹‹‹ ⦵⦵⦵ ››››

B ut we've only just arrived," I said. "And the great palace, don't you want to look at it?"

Another crowded passenger boat was about to cast off. We were the last to board before the gangway was pulled up.

We travelled, side by side, in silence, she gripping my hand so tightly it hurt, as though she feared that if she let go I would topple overboard.

The day had lost its vitality and grown warm and sultry, with a sickly yellow sun glimmering through cloud haze. The water no longer sparkled but appeared sluggish. A rowdy party on board were singing lustily and no doubt they would sing all the way from here down to the Isle of Dogs.

I wanted to share with Mother the burden of what I now knew about myself. But she would not speak.

I wanted to beg for reassurance that, at the times when I went away, I was not like that woman, that when I left my body unattended, it did not perform those terrible antics, did not thrash and writhe uncontrolled on the ground.

37

"Mother," I began tentatively, "when I was separated from you, I saw something. And I wondered—"

"You saw the swans?" Mother interrupted.

"No, not the swans."

"The barge with the big red sail?"

"No. A person," I said.

"That woman," she said.

"Something happened to her. People were watching."

Mother said sharply, "That woman had nothing to do with us."

"But is *she* like *me*?" I asked. "Am *I* like *her*? When I go away and lose time?"

She said nothing, but stared out at the slowly passing riverscape, luxuriant under a sullen sky.

"And if I am like that, what is to become of me?"

And still she wouldn't answer.

It was only when we reached the bleak room at Giddings's lodgings that she began to speak again, this time without my having posed any question.

"I didn't know," she said, falling back onto the chair with her hands up to her face. "I just didn't know what to say. Never, never will we go near that terrible place again. We should not have gone in the first place. I was warned it was unsafe to take you near water. It was only my own selfish impetuosity."

She began to weep about the danger of the water.

"But the water did us no harm, Mother," I said. I had not seen her cry in front of me before. And I did not understood what she was so upset about. Such a short time ago she had been so blithely gay talking of her dukes and countesses, so cheerfully maudlin thinking of our queen's sad widowhood.

"They said you'd grow out of it," she sobbed. "You haven't! And we mustn't ever let anyone know. People must not see."

I understood that she was talking of my madness.

"Mother, it's all right," I said, putting my hand out to her. "I know about it. Indeed, I believe I knew all along, perhaps without knowing what I knew. And just the other day somebody confirmed it for me."

"*What* somebody?" she sniffed. "And what did they tell you? How *could* anybody tell you anything? You don't know anybody."

"He revealed to me, how I am mad. So now I know. And it's far better, Mother, that I should."

I thought she would be pleased by my attempt at a calm and reasonable manner. Instead, she leaped up from the chair in a terrible fluster.

"No, Albert! You are *not* mad! You are not."

I replied, "You're only trying to cover up the truth because you don't like it."

"You are not mad!" she shouted. "Your informant is wrong."

"Mother, I know I am mad. Why else do you make me lock myself in, if not to ensure that nobody sees me? Why else would you keep me away from people? Why do you douse the fire when you go out? Why do you watch me so slyly all the time?"

"It is not because you are mad. Don't ever let anybody tell you that."

"Why do you want to lie and try to keep the truth from me?"

We began to argue, raising our voices higher and higher. She was first to compose herself, and when I, too, had finished repeating the same thing over and over again, how I knew that I was mad, she said softly:

"Albert, you may suffer from the same affliction as that poor creature at Hampton Court Palace, but you are not insane and never have been. If you were truly mad, you would not even know it yourself. If you were mad, you would not be able to read and write, to paint and count, and keep my accounts so well."

She dabbed at her eyes with her gaudy glove.

"Listen to me, Albert, please. The true lunatic is one whose attacks of insanity follow the phases of the moon, for that is the meaning of the word. Yours follow no such pattern. They are irregular and inexplicable and hitherto incurable, though I hope that soon we may find a solution."

"Mother, I *want* to be mad!" I said irrationally. "I *have* to be mad." I felt myself to have been cheated out of one state that I had almost got accustomed to, and had it replaced with another.

"You are not insane, but you have been crippled in another way."

"Crippled? No, I will never be crippled." The sound of the word made me cringe. It was as though I had been stabbed through the chest wall with a knife. I was gasping for breath. The pain was intolerable. It was far worse than madness. I knew about cripples, hunched and hideously deformed people.

I knew those Shakespeare stories. Noble Hamlet, Prince of Denmark, was mad but hideous. Richard the Third was crippled. If I was to become a cripple, there was no reason to live any more.

"Your crippling is not like that. Yours is known as the falling sickness."

"I don't want to have it. I don't want to fall to the ground, and writhe and utter horrible noises, and dribble, and lose control."

"There is no choice in the matter. That's all there is to it. And now, if you can hold your patience and your temper, I shall send down for the kettle and some coal."

It was Mr. Giddings himself who trudged up with the full coal-scuttle and who laid the grate and lit the fire. He had heard our shouting. He looked at me warily, as though expecting me to leap at him and tear his throat out. The rumour that I was a defective had spread throughout the building. He had given Mother a week before we had to be out, providing there was no further disturbance from me, in which case our departure must be sooner than a week.

After he had left us alone, we sat in silence sipping our tea on either side of the hearth, Mother on the chair, I on the blanket on the floor.

She said, "Now I shall tell you about yourself. You say you wish to hear only the truth. So here is one part of it. Once, we lived with your grandmother. She was an ugly woman. I can only hope you don't remember her. At least we were housed, but in the end I couldn't stand her tormenting any longer. She told me every day that, through you, I had been cursed and God was punishing me for what I'd done behind her back."

"For what *you'd* done!" I said. "But it's not *you* that has this thing!" Why should Mother be cursed when it was *my* curse?

"She was a hard woman, showed no sympathy for either of us. She said I must carry the shame of you till the end of my days. That the burden of you would drag me down even lower than I was. That's when I left. I had to prove

41

that I could do something with my life, not just hold on, but rise above it, go up in the world and take you with me."

I was glad to have an explanation of our nomadic and secretive way of life and Mother's perpetual endeavour to achieve genteel respectability.

"So does she know, how you are doing now?" I asked. "With all your pleasant pupils and good connections?" I was humouring her. Even in her pink bonnet, she could hardly be said to be much up in the world.

"She's long dead. And good riddance. Why, if she walked in now, and asked for a drink of water, I wouldn't even give her the time of day."

That night, I was back on the lumpy horsehair couch and Mother was back in the bed. Huddled under my crochet blanket, I suddenly found myself fully awake in the darkness and overcome with a sense of profound terror. So intense was my dread, I feared that I was falling into a fit, though there was no distortion of sound or vision.

Instead, I felt myself jolted to another time and place. I was sitting on a back-door step. A cold flagstone was beneath my buttocks and the morning sun shone brightly down onto my head. A large woman was seated before me on a little wooden stool over which her massive thighs flowed. She had her back to me and I could see the mounds of side-flesh rippling down from under her arms. She was immensely powerful. All around her were tubs of steaming water and soaking linen. She was a washerwoman. But she wasn't using her strength to wash the clothes. In one of her tubs she was drowning the kittens.

This was my memory of my grandmother when I had

lived with her. My place was there, seated behind her on a cold step, and I must not move for fear that her great muscled arm would lash out to remind me of my place.

I went to sleep sweating with terror and when I awoke to the new morning, it was not with the numbed confusion that followed one of my disappearances from the world. Instead, I felt joyful and refreshed to be alive, and living here alone with my mother in Mortlake.

I had seen her putting them into the water and holding their heads down under the water because they kept bobbing up. I knew what they were. I had seen them born in the shed. I knew how easily it might happen to me. I saw bubbles rising to the surface.

She did not even try to hide from me what she was doing, though when the other children came running over to see, she shooed them away. They were not to witness this extinction of life. But I was of no account.

After that, I lived with the fear that she would be rid of me as she had rid herself of the kittens. The she-cat had littered too often that season. They had to be put down.

I knew that I, too, was unwanted, though for some different reason which I hadn't yet understood. As I sat behind her, I begged in my four-year-old heart, Don't put me down. I am not useless and blind and mewing and defenceless like a baby kitten. I am useful. I can do things. See how useful I will be.

At night, I silently cried again, Don't put me down. Don't ignore me. Don't leave me. Don't forget me. Don't force my face under the water.

When the old woman went to fetch a washbag stuffed with soiled linen, I leaned forward and could see the four small shapes submerged in the tub. A fifth was not dead but floundering blindly over the bodies of its companions from the womb, trying to learn how to swim. Disobeying my grandmother, I got up and ran to the tub, fished out the living kitten and flung it far into the bush at the side of the yard. Then I quickly returned to my place on the step.

The following day, the other children found the body in the bush and gave it a proper funeral with wildflowers, and the old woman smiled and laughed and gave them biscuits.

Thanks to Giddings's boot-boy downstairs, Mother and I were allowed to remain at the lodgings. He told his master how Mother was a lady and would lend the crumbling establishment an air of decency, and that he himself would make it his business to ensure that I never escaped to cause trouble with other tenants. For a small fee, additional to our rent, he would be the turnkey.

Despite the episodes, which I now knew to be seizures, and which punctuated so many of the days, the time at Giddings's lodgings was one of the most placid periods of my life. Lawrie, for such was his name, was proud to have me as his own personal madboy. I was glad to have the quiet company of this gentle jailer.

Whenever he had time spare from his work, he came up to visit me. Hearing those great heavy hoofs clomping towards the door, I would feel my heart lift. If I was copy-painting, he would not disturb me but would sit and watch. We would talk a little and share what knowledge we had. I told him about volcanoes, Nine Men's Morris, and earthquakes. He told me tales of life in Water Lane, how he had once tried to run away with a travelling fair which passed by the end of the lane, but Giddings had caught him and dragged him back.

One of the happier stories he told me was of the eel-fairs he remembered from when he was small.

"Elver run they call it proper," he said. "But we call it Eel-fair. They was all three years old, same age as myself, and they come drifting in from the great oceans, little things no bigger than a piece of string. Put altogether they were like a big black rope all up the edge of the river. And everyone was dashing out with their buckets and bailing them out for eel pie. Herons liked them, too, if we didn't get there first. They don't come no more, so we can't do that now. I'd like them to come back."

"Perhaps they are being fished out further downstream?" I suggested. He thought about it, then shook his big head. "Don't believe it's that. Mr. Giddings says it's because the waterflow's too mucky. I don't think it's that, neither. I believe it's for they don't like the people round here no more."

When I had finished a painting, or had to let some part dry off, I would read to Lawrie from *The Illustrated London News* or we would play at cards or a board game.

One afternoon, after sitting silently for fifteen minutes, Lawrie informed me how his namesake was Lawrence.

"And he was a holy man that I was named after."

I said I wished I, too, had been named after a holy saint instead of after a royal consort from Germany.

Lawrie shook his big head. "No, it's not something to envy. My patron was burned to death on a red-hot iron griddle. And not one of them people standing by thought to douse the fire and save him. That was murder. Halfway through, he called out to his captors, 'Turn me over, brothers, for I am done on that side,' like he was a herring. I think of that every morning when I get up in the cold and that gives me strength, knowing my lot is never so tough as being baked alive."

"Who told you the story?"

"That's no story. That's all true."

"Who gave you the name, then?"

Lawrie had no idea. "But it weren't Old Giddings, and that's for sure."

Lawrie had neither mother nor father, and never had had so far as he could recall, nor was he interested in locating them. Then, as though afraid he might have offended me by his suggestion that mothers had no great use, he asked my opinion of their value. I explained that since I had experience of only one, my answer would be biased.

Lawrie said, "If ever I was obliged to have one, then I'd like one like yours. She's pretty as a flower, that one."

"Is she?" I said in surprise.

"Old Giddings says he wouldn't be surprised if someone didn't gather her up in a posy one of these days."

I said that, grateful as I was to have a mother, I much wished I had a brave patron to emulate, just as he had his saint. My own namesake had died, not in splendid martyrdom, nor even, as Mother liked to claim in her history recitation, of overwork from so faithfully serving his wife's people, but of intestinal infection from foul drains at his wife's castle, where fresh water and refuse flowed together along the same pipes.

Lawrie said, "So it's not only us poor folk must live with the stink. It's them up the top of the hill besides."

Lawrie thought for a week before he came up with an

46

idea. "If you're not so stuck on Albert, you should take another name."

"I cannot change my name," I said, shocked.

"That is not so," said Lawrie. "You may change anything you wish."

It seemed a strange idea, as though changing one's identity. I said, "Well, I have a middle name. Like the Prince of Wales, I am Albert first, then Edward."

Lawrie repeated it uncertainly. "We can but try and see how it works for you," he said.

Mother refused absolutely to go along with it. But in the company of my gentle jailer, I found myself growing calmer and stronger in spirit, no longer weakly Albert, the defective, but Edward, the copy-painter and tranquil prisoner.

All might have continued as it was had not Mother been so set on finding a cure.

"I am going to find one, I know I shall," she said.

And one afternoon she returned in a state of high excitement.

Five

"Albert, Albert! I have found a faith healer!"

"Mother, I have told you. My name is Edward."

"Don't be silly with all that when I have something important to say. Now, an acquaintance of the housekeeper at the Barkers', in whom I confided, has an introduction. This person was *most* interested to hear about you. He says he *can* cure you! He says miracles are taking place, throughout the world, every single day of the year."

She danced around the table with delight, clapped her hands, and embraced me tenderly.

"He is *quite* a gentleman and most keen to meet you."

Since I met no people, I, too, was keen. I wondered when I would be taken to meet him.

"He has said that he can meet only when the time is ripe. So we have to wait and see," said Mother.

It sounded curious and mysterious. Four days passed. Nothing happened until, on the following Sunday as we were walking back from church, which was almost my only permitted outing though still nobody there spoke to either Mother or to me, a man approached us on the street. He was somewhat shabbily dressed, the cuffs of his suit having seen better days, the spats over his shoes in need of a good cleaning. But he was well spoken.

"And good morning to you, madam," he said to Mother, raising his hat with a grand show of politeness. Next he shook me warmly by the hand, more as though he were greeting an old acquaintance than making a new one. Down and up, down and up went my arm in his firm grasp as if he thought he was working the long handle of a water-pump.

"God has told me that it is His intention to heal you of your sickness," he said, beaming at me.

Could I really believe that this thrusting stranger could do something for me?

"As a matter of fact, I am not sick in the usual manner—" I began, till I saw how Mother put her finger to her lips and shook her head to silence me.

"Can the Ethiopian change his skin, or the leopard his spots? Woe is me, my mother, that thou hast borne a man of strife and a man of contention to the whole earth?"

I was entirely unsure how to answer these questions until I realized that he was quoting, from memory, a passage of the Bible and that no direct response from me was required.

He said, "Madam, we have to wait for the signal from the Lord that the time has truly come. As soon as that signal comes I shall know it. When the Lord gives the word, I shall be hopping right along."

He seemed kindly and well-meaning.

"Albert, say thank you to Mr. Gosforth," said Mother.

I said, "The Lord speaks to you *directly*?" I had never heard of anyone, except Moses and possibly Lawrie, to whom this happened. "Are you a minister of the church?" He was wearing a purple silk shirt-front, somewhat in the manner of a bishop.

"As it were," said Mr. Gosforth, nodding and smiling.

Mother reminded him where we were lodged. Mr. Gosforth said he did not know the place but was sure that if this was what the Lord desired, he would be led to it.

I said, "I look forward to your visit," for at that point I really did. Even a man who pumped my arm and made unlikely claims of hearing God would be welcome.

"Except—" I faltered, "I very much hope you'll get the word at a time when my mother is home, as I am allowed to receive no visitors unless she is there."

I did not want to raise Mother's suspicions about Lawrie, the servant boy, who came and went whenever it suited us both.

I saw her vehemently shaking her head at me again. "Why no, Albert," she said. "In this special situation it will be perfectly all right for Mr. Gosforth to visit any moment he feels the time is ripe."

We heard nothing more of Mr. Gosforth for several weeks, during which time I had to mark only one black cross in my diary. This marked a seizure which, though unpleasant, was neither severe nor prolonged, its only enduring problem being that, in my fall, I injured my elbow on the fender. The wound became inflamed and Mother had to apply a linseed-meal poultice, so I was unable to work for a few days.

My flower paintings, or rather, Mother's flower paintings, for that is how they were sold, were increasing in popularity. My friendship with Lawrie was equally flourishing, though his tuition was of a very different order from Mother's.

He was watching me one afternoon, open-mouthed with admiration, as I painted a peony.

"Did you know, young Edward, that one day the tribespeople came hunting to the valley of our river?"

I said I did not, for I had no idea of what he was speaking.

It seemed he was referring to people of early history.

"They arrived one morning upriver, and nobody knew who they were."

He spoke as though their visit was quite recent.

I said, "Lawrie, if you mean the primeval hunters, that was before the time of Saint Lawrence, longer ago in time than man can count."

This meant nothing to Lawrie, for, as I was beginning to discover, although he knew plenty about eels and water-life, he was unable to count beyond eight and sometimes only six.

"Oh yes, Edward, it was well before that. And when they came they didn't even know the name of our river. They didn't even know the power of the steam engine, or how to build a bridge."

"Yes, they were primitive people."

"And they ate blackberries. You can find ample blackberries by the river. Also water lettuce. Though they would not have known the best place for that unless someone had showed them first."

Lawrie's sense of time and space was different from my own. In many ways, his was so much safer, for thousands of years of river history were compressed into a dot with which we were all in touch. It made my own misfortune seem less significant and far easier to bear.

I was copying Madonna lilies with a complicated background of trailing ivy, which turned out to be much easier than it first looked, when Lawrie unlocked the door. But instead of settling himself on the window ledge to watch, he announced in a strangely formal voice that there was a fellow downstairs wanting to come up and should he send him off with a flea in his ear?

"It's all right, brother," I said, for Lawrie and I had taken to claiming between ourselves that we were brothers. "If he is a talkative gentleman with a purple shirt-front, then I know who he is. You may show him up. He's a man come to cure me."

"You mean, so you won't be mad?" My newly claimed brother seemed disappointed.

"I believe so."

I had not attempted to explain to Lawrie that, according to Mother, I was not in fact insane, but subject to a different kind of disorder which made me sometimes *appear* to be mad; for I had begun to discover that with Lawrie some concepts were beyond his grasp.

However satisfactorily I might think I had explained them, no matter how hard he had tried, he could not understand abstract ideas, such as time or money. Despite my tuition, he still could not count money, knowing only that a guinea was untold wealth and a farthing was enough to buy one egg, yet having no idea that twenty-one shillings made up the guinea, and that four farthings together added up to one penny. Being unable to count reliably beyond six, he couldn't know that there were habitually seven days in a week, and twelve months to a year. And this was why he spoke of Saint Lawrence and the primeval men as though they had lived but a short while ago.

When Mr. Gosforth made his entrance to our room, he seemed momentarily taken aback. He said, "Is this all?"

I was baffled. "All of what, sir?"

Mr. Gosforth addressed himself to Lawrie, who lurked in the doorway. "All they have as their place of residence? Just the single room here?"

Perhaps he had been deceived by Mother's pleasant manners into misunderstanding our situation.

Lawrie said, "This is a good room. Look, they have the separate recess for madam's bed. Downstairs you can see bad rooms." Lawrie himself had no room, nor even a bed of his own. He slept on a heap of corn sacks in the kitchen.

Mother returned then, flustered to find Mr. Gosforth there.

"Dear lady, so many apologies, for not having visited sooner. I was waiting for the word, and the Lord has now sent His message, clear as crystal water flowing from the holy mountain."

Sometimes Mother's hope was infectious. I had begun to believe the claims that the man could cure me. Ever since he entered the room, my hands had been clammy with anticipation. Now foolish Mother held up the procedure by darting about like a waterflea, tidying up things that did not need to be tidied, asking whether he wished her to send the boy for tea or some other beverage, where he wished to sit, which, given that there was but the one chair, on which he had already seated himself in the centre of the room, seemed unnecessary.

Grandly he waved away all offers. He was as keen as I to start. Mother asked if she should leave us alone.

"Why no, dear madam. It is of the essence that you remain. But the servant must go."

Mother closed the door on Lawrie. I hoped he would follow events through the keyhole.

Mr. Gosforth began his cure by drawing me to him as he sat on the chair and staring into my face. At first I stared back, but I found the red veins on his nose, and the fleshy lips, disconcerting.

After some moments of silence, Mr. Gosforth announced that I had had a serious fall on my head when I was young. "And this is the chief cause of all his suffering."

Mother looked bemused. "That can't be right," she said. "That first seizure he ever took, he was less than one day old. It shook the life out of the midwife, but the baby didn't fall. Of that I can be sure."

Mr. Gosforth repeated in a flat expressionless tone, "As an infant, the boy had a most serious fall."

I was intrigued by both the pronouncement and by Mother's denial. She spoke so rarely of my childhood that I might almost not have had one.

"Because of his delicate condition, I was always careful," she insisted. "It's true that he's taken many falls and knocks *since* infancy, but it has always been clear that these have been as a *result* of the falling sickness, rather than the cause.

The physician I consulted when the boy was eight assured me that his condition was not brought about by neglect or any fault of mine."

Abruptly, Mr. Gosforth changed the subject. He talked about the forthcoming visit of the Prince of Wales to attend the regatta, and speculated on which members of the prince's set were likely to be accompanying him.

I wished him to get on with the business. Instead, he told Mother of all the important people who had benefited from his healing.

"And I have been called to attend to members of the royal family, you understand. And to help members of the Cabinet. In addition to my healing powers, I have the special knowledge, denied to most people. Let me give you an example of my clairvoyancy. I can see that you, dear madam, have a close friend who is sick and causing you much worry. She, too, is a teacher, of elocution."

Mother smiled and shrugged. Mr. Gosforth started on another line of enquiry.

"Aha! Now I sense that you are missing someone very badly." He was not looking at Mother but was staring straight ahead as in a trance. "No, it is not a *person* you are missing. It is your *home* that you are missing. Which home is it that you are missing?"

Mother said quite firmly, "*This* is our home. We aren't missing any other place."

But I liked the idea of having a sweet special place called home that one might miss.

"You are, I perceive, homesick for your parents' place," said Mr. Gosforth.

Mother looked irritated. "My mother is dead," she said

sharply. She was growing impatient. "All this roundabout talk is stopping you from getting on with the intended purpose of your visit."

Mr. Gosforth sat silently for a few seconds with his eyes closed. "Your true home, which you are missing, is heaven. That is the place that you should be missing. And by distancing yourself from heaven, you are jeopardizing your son's health. You have ceased to read the Bible!"

Mother accepted this accusation. "It is true that I do not read often. But that is because I have to go out teaching in order to support us."

"There, you have it! The moment we stop the constancy of our habits, these things come upon us."

Despite my apprehension about this graceless man, I did so want his claims to be true. I wanted him to be trustworthy.

I considered the awful possibility that so simple a thing as Mother's failure to read her Bible enough could have caused all my suffering. Then I thought of Lawrie, just the other side of the door, who could scarcely read his own name, let alone the Bible, yet put all his naive faith in Saint Lawrence on the grill. Was he doomed to suffer some terrible affliction?

"But, Mr. Gosforth," I burst out, "what of the hundreds of people who don't know how to read? And what about all the boys who are not afflicted as I am and whose mothers read the Bible even less than mine does?"

Mr. Gosforth had his answer, though he directed it not to me but to Mother. "Different criteria are set by God for every individual. Then again, maybe it is not you, but your parents or grandparents who are to blame, for a man's sins are visited unto the third and fourth generation. However, this is no time to get wrapped up in dogma. We have now concluded the first part of the process. And we must move on."

For the second stage of the process, Mr. Gosforth asked for our Bible to be placed in his hands.

Mother fetched her New Testament from beneath the pillow on the bed.

Mr. Gosforth seemed displeased with it. With a sigh, he took from his own pocket a small Bible, containing both Old and New Testaments, and rifled through the pages, muttering to himself.

"Genesis? No. Not Genesis. Daniel? Yes? No. Aah, here we have Jeremiah."

Mr. Gosforth handed the book to Mother, indicating the passage she was to read.

"Wouldn't it be wiser for Albert himself to read, since he is the subject of the healing?"

Mr. Gosforth seemed uncertain about the wisdom of this. "The boy reads?" he said doubtfully.

Mother handed me the book anyway.

The passage was not from Jeremiah but from Ezekiel. *"The fathers have eaten sour grapes,"* I read. *"And the children's teeth are set on edge."*

As I continued, Mr. Gosforth was nodding and smiling to himself, not that there was much in his chosen verses to smile about.

"See, madam, how the miracle is already beginning!" He seemed astounded at my fluency. "The intellect returns."

"Mr. Gosforth, sir, I am not suffering from loss of intellect," I said. "And never have."

57

"Quite so."

Mr. Gosforth next demanded a cup of cold water.

Mother fetched the water-carafe. "But would you not prefer tea, or a cordial?"

"No. Just plain water. But it must be freshly drawn. It is not for me to drink. I require the liquid of life for the third and final part of the mystical process."

Lawrie, conveniently close to hand outside, was despatched.

Mother and Mr. Gosforth waited in an apprehensive silence while Lawrie clattered downstairs, Mr. Gosforth staring up at the ceiling, Mother staring down at the floor.

From the window, I watched Lawrie emerge into the yard below. I waved. He smiled up, pleased to be able to participate in the ritual.

Giddings's washerwoman was squatting beside the pump with her tub of suds and heaps of dirty sheets, and had to shuffle aside to let Lawrie have his turn. I saw the splash and slurp as he swung vigorously on the handle. As the washerwoman waited for him to finish, she looked up at the window and scowled at me. I knew that everybody in the building despised me for what I was.

When Lawrie reappeared with the brimming jug and a beaming smile, Mr. Gosforth took the vessel in his left hand and ordered me to stand before him. He placed his right hand over my eyelids so that they were closed, and sprinkled my forehead with drops. This startled me, as I wasn't expecting it. Some dribbled down my neck, which alarmed me because I knew that wearing a damp collar can cause fainting, haemorrhoids, liver chills, and all manner of ailments. Mr. Gosforth began to pray, and I could only trust that the damp would not do me lasting damage.

When he began the Lord's Prayer, he indicated we were to join in. Lawrie's hoofs shuffled uneasily. He knew no prayers by heart, but muttered some nonsensical incantations.

Mr. Gosforth's memory was failing him, too, for when he began to recite the Twenty-third Psalm, he faltered with the words by the fourth verse, and Mother and I had to complete it for him.

Finally, Mr. Gosforth anointed my eyes with the cold water in the jug, then my ears, my temples, and the inside of my wrists. He asked me to roll up my right sleeve. He was taken aback by the bandage on my elbow and asked in a tone of some indignation what it covered.

"He took a fall," said Mother, "and unluckily caught his elbow on the corner of the fender. It is taking its time to heal."

"Remove the bandage," Mr. Gosforth ordered. "You will never, never wear it again."

It was unclear if this was an order or a prediction. But in any case, he was visibly upset by the rawness of the wound and took hold of my forearm gingerly. He make stroking movements down the arm to the tips of the fingers, then pulled each digit, one by one, to their ends as though extending them. This was repeated on my left arm.

"The evil influences are being drawn away," he explained.

If indeed I was full of evil, the sensation of it being drawn away by Mr. Gosforth's hands seemed soothing.

As his voice droned on, I let my gaze wander through the window to the warehouses opposite. Between them, I noticed that just where Mother had first spotted the green of a tree, there was indeed a river view, a tiny triangular glimpse of sulky brown water ruffled by a breeze.

The fact that I had noticed this for the first time this day at this moment I knew to be an omen for good. The river that carried away the effluent from the brewery, the industrial wastes and dyes from the carpet factory, the grey sedimented suds from the washerwoman's tub, would now wash away all the foul wickedness that was in me.

"Oh, cleanse me of these sins, please, river," I found myself praying aloud.

"Amen," said Mr. Gosforth.

He handed the jug to Mother and commanded her to take a sip of the water in which his big grubby hands had dabbled. She obeyed reluctantly.

He ordered me to finish off the remainder and told Mother that I was to be dosed that evening with cod liver oil mixed with an equal quantity of honey.

"The ritual is now complete," he declared, in such a loud voice that I saw poor Lawrie give a start. "The boy has been cleansed. The healing will begin immediately."

I felt elated.

"The Lord saw fit to afflict the boy with the painful burden, and the Lord now sees fit to unyoke him. I shall return to offer further treatment if the Lord instructs me. Meanwhile, I shall be praying."

"How do you feel, Albert?" Mother asked.

"Exceedingly well," I said, and she hugged me tightly.

"How can we thank you, Mr. Gosforth, for giving up your time?" Mother spread her hands helplessly, with the moisture of gratitude brightening her eyes.

"This is all the work of the Lord," murmured Mr. Gosforth. "I neither expect, nor accept, repayment. However, a small gesture of appreciation when it expresses your honest sentiment is entirely acceptable, whether a guinea, or half a guinea. For the Lord's work is never done."

Embarrassment crossed Mother's face. She had no more than a threepenny bit in her purse. However, the surge of gratitude was so strong that she unpinned the brooch from the lapel of her jacket. It was only cheap tin, set with a piece of pink glass. She loved the colour pink.

"Why no, no, my dear lady," said Mr. Gosforth. "Never in my life could I accept anything so valuable, so deeply personal."

So Mother did not persist in offering it. But as she began to refasten it, Mr. Gosforth leaned forward and took it from her after all.

"Since you insist on offering up this widow's mite, it would be churlish to spurn your gesture."

He pocketed it quickly without any remark and made for the door.

"Albert, say thank you to Mr. Gosforth."

I subjected my arm to the water-pump technique again, the vigour of which almost shook me out of the relaxed calm I had been in.

Mother waved him off down the stairs. "Thank you, thank you, kind Mr. Gosforth."

And he called back, "Should you wish to donate to the Lord's good work, I will be happy to forward funds to an appropriate source, where they can be used for the maximum benefit of mankind."

"Oh, I shall, I shall," said Mother. "Just as soon as I see how well Albert is, I shall come round immediately to tell you."

How much, how terribly much we both wanted the healing to be true.

Six

*M*other administered the fish oil stirred with
honey, even though I protested at its vile
cloying taste, and I was without seizure for
the remainder of that day. I slept well that
night. I dreamed myself, not into a washerwoman's yard,
but to a quiet evening valley in which grew grape vines and
cypress trees, though I had seen neither. The dream landscape
stretched gently towards an expanse of blue water lapping
softly against a rocky shore, and I knew it to be the
sea, though I had never in my life seen it. A gentle warmth
all round told me I was in some foreign place.

I woke refreshed. There had been no night attack and I
was without a seizure for the whole of the next day, and the
one after that. I saw how Mother watched me carefully, and
I, too, was silently thrilled.

For all his strangeness, Mr. Gosforth was no charlatan.

Privately, I turned the pages of the red hide diary, marvelling
at the purity of the passing days, each unblemished by
the black ink cross.

"We must send word," Mother said. "To let him know that his wonderful healing has worked. And I shall, of course, apologize to him for my initial doubt. As soon as I get my money from the Barkers, we'll take him a donation."

I was confident, too confident. Never had I felt so full of life and vigour. I was normal.

Mother sent Lawrie round to Mr. Gosforth with a message that we would shortly be calling on him.

On Saturday afternoon, the High Street was bustling with activity.

"Albert, there is something I wish to show you," Mother said, smiling as she made an unexpected yet deliberate detour off our route and into a narrow side street lined with small but busy shops, a silversmith, a fabric merchant, a stationer's, *Dukes & Sons, Printers and Stationers of Repute, est. 1774, retail and trade suppliers, personal and marriage stationery, finest engraving. Quality our specialty.*

This was where she had been bringing the flowers.

"I noticed their special window only last week, quite by chance, and hoped they would keep it out long enough for you to see it, too."

She led me towards the bow-fronted shop window. Each side was taken up with everyday merchandise, samples of manila envelopes, watermarked writing-paper, business cards and business writing-paper, flyers and printed handbills, while in the centre was mounted a colourful and appealing display of newfangled fancy goods, so arranged that the casual passerby could not help but be drawn irresistibly towards it.

There were printed picture scraps for screens and scrap

albums, hanging calendars with silk tassels, decorated paper mourning gloves, ladies' visiting cards, Chinese lanterns, and pretty paper fans bearing finely printed decorations and tender messages. It was a visual feast.

And at the very centre, as the focal point, was the peony that I had so painstakingly painted, but it was not just one peony, but the same one reproduced many times over. Each one had been mounted on card with an embossed paper-lace border, and further embellished with the application of a tiny satin bow.

I peered closely through the window and saw how it had lost little of its bright clarity in the printing process. Even though the design bore no signature, neither mine nor Mother's, it was definitely our flower. In the display, there were other flower pictures, but most of them so crudely painted that they might as well have been coloured cabbages as the asters or larkspurs they were endeavouring to represent.

"Well," said Mother, taking my hand in hers and giving it a squeeze. "What do you think of that, then?"

I nodded appreciatively.

To see our work on public show like this was a proud moment, even without any recognition that we had done it.

"And he wants more, Albert," said Mother. "Plenty more, if we can do them. He's given me some new samples to work from. Anemones, Christmas roses. I believe he'll take as many as we can do!"

She grabbed me round the waist and waltzed me down to the next lamppost and round it, then back to where we had started from, ignoring the pedestrians who had to step aside to give us space for our dance of triumph.

Arm in arm and slightly breathless, we proceeded in a more stately progress down the lane, stopping now and then to peer into another shop window to choose things we might buy when we had grown rich on painted flowers. Mother chose a cut-glass decanter and an ormolu carriage clock to go on the mantelpiece in her dream drawing-room. I lingered in front of the cloth merchant where the window was stacked with bolts of shiny silks and rich brocades in vermilion, azure green, peacock blue.

"I'd have some stuff from in here," I said.

"You strange child. Whatever would you do with furnishing fabric?"

I said, "I like the colours."

I would hang them upon the walls so that when the light shone on them, the jewel colours would glow.

We reached the end of the alley. As we turned back into the High Street, a gas lamp bowed down towards me, pinning me to the ground, and a coal-hole cover on the pavement leered up. The taste of metal came onto my tongue. I had been here before, seen all this before.

"Help me, Mother, catch me," I tried to say. But it was too late.

It was days before I was fit enough to cross the room and take up my place at the painting table.

I had just begun painting again when I took two more bad seizures in quick succession. The second of these was most especially galling for the serious destruction it caused, not to my person but to my created work.

I had nearly completed a bouquet of lily-of-the-valley. Even Mother admitted that they were the nearest to perfection I had yet achieved. Alone with them, I almost felt I could smell the fragrant scent as they grew on some shady woodland bank, each delicate cap-flower as white as snow, each spearlike leaf as bright as limes.

I added a sparkling drop of dew on the frilled edge of one of the blossoms, then pulled back in the chair to judge the effect before placing the picture safely out of the way and beginning preparations for the next. This was to be of a sprig of orange blossom, doubtless for a marriage card, set against a trellis of rustic wood.

The onset was so sudden I had no time to consider what would happen when I fell across the table onto the paint palettes, the water jar, and the ink bottle with its cap open.

I descended immediately into the deep dark vortex of death, and centuries later crawled back up on the far side of life.

It was only much later that I came to discover what I had destroyed. The lily-of-the-valley was scarred across the centre with a waterful of ink. Hours of work, days of work, had been all for nothing.

"I done what I could, Edward," Lawrie told me, for it was he who had found me first. "To help clear it up. But it's no good. It can't be saved."

"Why do you call him Edward when his name is Albert?" said Mother irritably.

It was two weeks before I was fit to go out. And on the very first day that Mother escorted me for a short walk to feel the air, by some awful coincidence, Mr. Gosforth was also about. He bore down upon us.

"Aha, strangers, who have been hiding like shadows beneath the rock!" He raised his hat to Mother. I noticed a rich heavy smell, not unlike that of the communion wine, emanating from him as he spoke.

"I was impatient to hear from you, for the Lord has sent me some more important information. He tells me to warn you that your son must acquire a small pocket-sized Bible, like this one, and must carry it *always* with him." From his own pocket he took a miniature volume little larger than the size of a postage stamp.

Mother tried to draw away from him. So he turned his attention from her to me, reaching out to hold my hand.

"Ah, the dear child, look how well he is. In fine youth-exuberant form!"

"Excuse me, Mr. Gosforth, but Albert and I have to be on our way," said Mother.

"But here is God, telling you one single thing that you should do to secure the boy's health. If you are not prepared to obey Him, then I should not be at all surprised if the fits don't return to plague him further."

I feared the threatening tone of his voice. I felt we should do whatever he asked.

"Return?" snorted Mother. "How do you say, *return?* They never went. I have been living with them since the day he was born. Your interference has only made them worse. Come along now, Albert."

But Mr. Gosforth was holding my hand and I could not pull away.

"Sin is the cause of all disease, all ill health, whether it is a disease of the body or of the mind. Sin lies in the resistance and pride of mankind in refusing to obey the word of God, and to do the simple things God wants. The devil is come down unto you, having great wrath, because he knoweth that he hath but a short time. And that is the revelation of Saint John."

He grew excited, words and quotations tumbling from his fat lips along with a spray of foamy spit.

"You're mad!" said Mother. "Insane. You talk in riddles. Let him go now."

"Riddles? Ah no. These are not riddles but sayings of the holy book, which you ignore at your peril."

Mother pulled on my hand to try to free me from his hold.

Mr. Gosforth held on more tightly. "From now on, the word of God must be where you can touch it with your hand." He raised my hand in his and touched it against the tiny Bible in his breast pocket. "It must go with you exactly as God said. 'Let the word go with you.' It is because of the special sin that has been invested in you, that you need more than ritual cleansing. Remember, boy, dead flies cause the ointment of the apothecary to send forth a stinking savour."

Mother managed to release my hand and, wrapping me within the protective folds of her cape, ran with me down the street.

Mr. Gosforth pursued us, waving his arms, screaming.

"Don't you even *want* the Lord to give him back his goodness? I beg you to hear me out. You are treading a dangerous path if you ignore the words of God."

I was shaken by the encounter, though once we were away from him, with his foul breath no longer blowing in my face, and his grasp on my hand, I wondered if I had lost my only chance of a cure.

Mother was not shaken, only annoyed.

"Did you notice," she said, "that he wore *spats*? I should have remembered never to trust a man in spats."

"Why not?"

"Your father wore spats."

I wondered if I was a love-child. But I did not dare ask. Besides, she would doubtless give me an answer that suited her mood rather than the truth.

Despite the failings of Mr. Gosforth, Mother's optimism that somewhere there was a proper cure, either miracle or scientific, did not falter. She heard talk of a mesmerist, of an Italian hypnotist, of a woman in Wapping who had invented a cold-water cure, and of a doctor in London who specialized in my condition.

"But he is very costly."

We would have to treble or even quadruple the number of paintings I completed.

"So we will try the others first."

The seizures came and went, and came back, with no apparent rhythm. They increased in frequency and decreased, with or without fish oil and praying. The people in the rest of the world, as I viewed them from the dusty window, proceeded with their busy lives while the number of black crosses in my red diary increased till it was more like a full graveyard.

And my body was like the battleground, marked with the humiliating signs of defeat. During every fit I got bruised, and bumped, grazed, cut, scratched, jolted, broken, or shaken, according to how I fell, from what height, and against which piece of furniture, or doorknob, bannister railing, bed-end, or fire-guard I landed.

Mother's great fear was that I might tumble through an open window and break my neck, or onto an open fire and burn to death. For this reason, the windows were kept closed, and the fire was doused with cold ash whenever she went out.

My own fear was that I might fall while holding an open penknife or a pair of paper-cutting scissors and that the blade of either would pierce the palm of my hand, rendering me unable to draw and paint. And now there was this additional fear that, in falling, I would damage more of our livelihood.

However, I became aware that there was a simple means by which I could at least lessen some of the injuries I inflicted on myself.

I recognized that, though the onset of an attack was rapid and came upon me unexpectedly, there was in fact a brief period of warning before the seizure took full hold and I lost consciousness. These few terrible moments were, in their way, one of the worst parts of each episode.

During this time, which was only seconds long yet felt like centuries, I would feel overwhelmed by an oppressive sense of dread that something tremendously awful was about to occur. There would be pressure in the air as though the massive oak beams of heaven's ceiling were about to come crashing down through space. There was a high-pitched screaming and whining as if all the noises on earth had been invited to sing together in one cacophonous choir, their music rising to an unbearable pitch that would split open my eardrums.

The light, even if it was only the faint gleam of a single candle, grew in intensity so that there was no shade behind my eyes, only a blinding brightness which burned into my swimming brain. There was the strange taste of metal on my tongue and the nauseous smell of burning hair in my nostrils. And overall was the premonition of impending doom about which I could do nothing, only submit to the inevitable horror.

All this occurred with little time to call out for help, to reach the bed, to loosen my collar, but was just time enough, if only I could master myself, to step back from a sharp fender, to drop the open pen-knife, to move away from the glass window, to slide down from the chair to the relative safety of the floor.

Often, I found myself so frozen by the confusion and distortion of all natural senses that I was unable to move at all.

"This is the falling sickness!" I would try to tell myself. "You have only seconds to act. Do it now. You are not dying. This is only the falling sickness. Drop the pen. Drop the knife. Get down. Get down. Down. Down."

Lawrie, meanwhile, continued as my chief companion. Even though he was always the strong warder and I the invalid captive, I felt much affection for him.

One afternoon during a peaceful half hour I painted his portrait. It was a miniature in watercolour on the margin of a larger sheet of cartridge paper that had been trimmed down to the required size for a camellia.

I had just completed a delicate moss rose accompanied by dainty blue forget-me-nots and was disinclined to begin a complete new study immediately.

Lawrie seemed intrigued that I should want to paint him. Although he agreed willingly, he found it hard to remain in a pose. Every few seconds, he darted over to observe the progress of his face as it emerged from the blank paper like a reflection in a still pool.

"It is not a flower, is it?" he said. "That is a young man, looking out."

It was as though it was the first time he had ever thought of himself as having any recognizable appearance that could be captured in this way.

"If you stand behind me like that, brother," I said, "I cannot capture you at all. You need to be in front of me, where I can see you."

"But if I can see you, even when I am downstairs and you are up here, why can you not see me when I am just behind you?"

It was a good likeness, perhaps too good to be kind, for as well as the bright red cheeks and coppery tousled hair, it showed the reality of his bulging misshapen cranium, the passive droop of his mouth, and the vacancy of his stare when his mind was at rest.

As soon as it was done to my satisfaction, I handed it to him. He seemed overcome and looked at it without saying anything for several minutes so that I feared he was upset at seeing his strange ugliness revealed. But then he bent forward and kissed the picture as reverently as if it were a holy relic before handing it back.

"No, it's for you," I said. "To keep. If you would like it."

His surprise and gratitude were apparent. He could not have looked more pleased if I had given him the moon and the sun and a bucketful of fresh eels.

I said, "As soon as the paint is dry, I'll mount it on a piece of card for you."

I was surprised at the discovery that I had the skill to capture more than just the likeness of flowers with my skill. I resolved to try a miniature of Mother as soon as she had the time to sit for me.

"Oh, Edward, my brother," said Lawrie. "You are the very best friend I ever had. Better even than my Saint Lawrence. And even when you're gone far away, I'll think of you every morning." And he flung his arms around my neck, nearly knocking me flying.

"But I am not planning on going away so long as Mr. Giddings does not throw us out," I said.

I had never before been hugged by another person, apart from Mother. I was startled.

"One day when I am rich, I shall buy a gilt frame for it, too," I said, for a watercolour painting needs protection if it is not to spoil.

Lawrie said, "Don't you worry about a frame. I shall always take care of this."

And before I could stop him, he had carefully folded the little painting, with the delicate brushstrokes still damp, over in half, then in half again, then a third time, and when it was tightly creased into a tiny rectangle about the size of Mr. Gosforth's miniature Bible, he tucked it in his pocket.

"Now it's safe and I shall keep it with me always. Thank you. Every time I look at it, I'll think of you because it was you that gave it to me."

Quite unintentionally, he had ruined the first portrait I had ever painted. But instead of anger, I felt more than ever that his simple innocence needed my protection, though the truth was that we both needed each other. I depended on him as my lifeline to the outside world. Lawrie conveyed to

74

me all the useful information about the everyday goings-on in the world.

It was he who came pounding up the stairs in great excitement one day with entirely unexpected news.

"Edward, my friend, my dearest brother! You are to gain a father!" he shouted, half laughing, half crying. The weeping won and he flung himself face-down on the old ottoman and beat the dusty stuffing with his fists. "She is to marry. And you will go away. I shall never see you again."

Seven

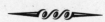

*M*y mother announced her plans somewhat differently.

"Albert, I have accepted to do something which is to change our lives forever. We are launching out into an exciting venture. I admit I am doing it in part for myself, but also for you so that you may have security. I think you will be very pleased with my decision. Can you guess what it is that we are to do?"

I chose not to. So she had to tell me.

"Mr. Bittern and I are to be married."

"Mr. Bittern?"

"Yes. I told you. I met him at the Barkers', for he is friendly with the housekeeper. He has agreed to take me as his wife. And you as his own son."

It seemed an unlikely arrangement.

Mr. Bittern was younger than my mother and pleasant enough, if in a somewhat distant yet fussy way. I did not believe he even noticed my presence when we met in the entrance hall of the Girls' Academy of Learning. This was probably an advantage, since I wore, that day, a bruised left cheekbone and a cut on my upper lip. Both were healing but were nonetheless evident.

I tried my best to be humble and polite to the man. But I knew little about marriage and love.

I was astounded at the rapidity of events. Mr. Bittern made arrangements for the ceremony to take place with as few delays as possible.

He applied to the bishop for a marriage by special licence so as to avoid the delay which the publishing of the Banns would have necessitated.

The reason for his haste was more a fear of losing his employment than the urgency of gaining the devotion of my mother. He was bursar at the school. His first wife having died, it was held by the governors of the Academy to be unsuitable for him to remain in his post, which was residential, in his current single state. The school had been endowed by a philanthropic duchess to educate forty local girls between the ages of seven and fourteen.

The bursar's acquisition of a wife was seen to be beneficial to all, particularly when it was learned that she could give tuition in fine drawing, singing, some conversational French, without requiring any extra remuneration beyond that the bursar himself received.

I said to my mother that it was fortunate I was so adaptable and used to these constant moves.

It had been her intention to leave me behind with the luggage to be collected later that evening. But Mr. Giddings knew a good trick when he saw one.

"Yes, missus," he said. "And I've got a bit of string with a hole in it," by which he meant that it would cost her a day and a night's extra rent, plus supervision fees, if I remained on the premises after midday, for although I took up less space than one tin trunk and two initialed pigskin bags, I was likely to be a good deal more trouble.

"That boy's hair grows through his head. So you know well enough, missus, what I mean by trouble," he said to my mother with a knowing nod at me, followed by a demonstration involving him rolling his eyes and hanging his tongue out. He did not go so far in his mimicry of me having a seizure as to urinate.

"Thank you, Mr. Giddings. But this is not a music hall," said my mother.

So we moved on from Mortlake, where the river was wide and flat and flowing slowly, to new pastures in a paradise called Isleworth a few miles upriver. It was in another county and an altogether different world.

"A charming village of some antiquity," said my mother as we bowled briskly along in a hansom cab towards her wedding and our new life. "And known in Queen Elizabeth's time as Thistleworth. It's all such lovely green fields and shining pools."

This time, she spoke the truth. We were moving to a place of pastoral tranquillity, where lush meadows ambled down to the river, and where the lapping tide came to meet the grass, where piebald cows stood all day in a profusion of golden buttercups, and where market gardens produced abundant pears and cantaloupes, peaches and nectarines for the dinner tables of the London well-to-do.

"I believe you will fall in love with the place as I already have. And so conveniently close to Richmond for our shopping," said my mother. "Even if Isleworth is said to be on the wrong side of the river for royalty."

For the marriage she wore her perky Sunday bonnet, freshly trimmed with cotton carnations which bobbed as she moved. Her cheeks quickly flushed the same colour as the fabric petals so that she looked as though she was over-heating with a fever. But she seemed in fine humour, laughing and giggling like a person half her age.

I supposed that the flush must be love and I felt quite shy to see her. During the ceremony, at which only two others besides myself and the priest were present, I kept my head down and my presence inconspicuous. However, I listened attentively, for I was much interested in the wording. The rector, robed in a billowy white surplice and apparently unaware of my mother's age, proclaimed firmly how the holy estate of matrimony was ordained primarily for the procreation of children, when as I already knew, in this particular instance, it was to secure the bursar's post.

The rector went on to state how matrimony was also a remedy against sin so that those who have not the gift of continency might keep themselves undefiled.

Though I had no wish to procreate children, I felt that marriage might be in my own interests as soon as I was old enough as a remedy against the sin with which I was still awash.

My mother and the bursar then promised to love and cherish one another until death, which seemed greatly to my own advantage as it ensured my security for some time.

The ceremony being over, the rector shook my mother's and the bursar's hands. We then all walked the half mile to the school, where we were invited into the principal's morning-room for a thimbleful of madeira and a slice of seed cake.

I tried to keep myself in the shadows. But the rector turned cheerfully to where I lurked beside a glass-fronted cupboard in the corner. Inside the cupboard was a collection of china figurines.

"So you must be pleased as Punch on a fine day with this amorous business, young lad?" he said. "All there and a ha'porth over, eh?"

I might have replied that I was so astonished by it all that I had not yet had time to consider my own feelings. But it seemed wiser to say nothing. I smiled and he patted me on the head. I held the tiny tot of madeira and stared at the cupboard. The glass front had a bevelled edge which caught the light to make dazzling rainbows across my vision. The figurines on the shelves inside had ugly painted faces which began to leer towards me.

"So you'll be seeing quite a few changes to your young life then?" the rector went on. "Nice place to come and live. I'll wager you have the time of your life. Pretty girls all over the place."

I busied myself with the dainty bone china plate and the dry sliver of seed cake.

He was determined to talk. "Be off to school soon, I dare say? Most rewarding days of a chap's life, as I remember, eh? M'sister's boy has just started Eton. He's a tug and is she proud of him!"

I did not know what a tug was.

"Scholarship boy, lad, King's Scholar. Bit too much of a slack-bob, if you ask my advice, not that anybody did. Won't play cricket, won't row. What's the meaning in life if a chap won't row, that's what I say."

A crumb of the dry seed cake became stuck in my throat and I began to choke. The rector slapped me heartily on the back between the shoulder blades.

"Choke away, boy. The churchyard's near!"

I knew what was going to happen. I ceased choking and gulped. I felt myself swallowing repeatedly. I saw my hands holding the china plate and the tiny glass of madeira, and they were out of proportion. There was no feeling in them. They were numb and starting to grow tight. Then all of a sudden I could see them beginning to shake.

As I was going down into the blackness to the music of tinkling china, I saw the faces that turned like gasping fish and I knew that my mother had not told any of them, least of all the young widower, her skinny beau, about the falling sickness.

And then nothing.

And nothing.

From that day of my arrival at the Academy, all members of the busy institution, whether teachers, or administrators, or domestics, knew of my shameful condition. It was as though I carried some foul odour.

Outdoors, the under-gardener averted his eyes so as not to catch my gaze directly. Indoors, the housemaids stepped aside in the corridors to let me pass. The principal avoided having to see me at all by informing my mother that I was excused attendance at Morning Prayers, even though it was compulsory for everybody else, from the dancing master down to the tweeny maid. I had been demoted so that now I was even lower than the servants.

"It is advisable for you to keep to the security of your own room," the bursar told me. "And not wander about at will. That way, you will cause the least upset."

"Am I not to receive any lessons?"

"You know you are not fit for it."

I had been expecting to benefit, if only partially, from such teaching as might be available or suitable for me.

"It would be unwise," said the bursar, "even unkind, to lead you towards expectations which can never be fulfilled. Furthermore, to educate cripples beyond their needs is dangerous to their nature, to their prospects, and to society."

So I left the seclusion of my room only when I knew the bursar was securely in his office.

"Well, just look what's here!" said the tweeny when she found me skulking near the pantry door. "Large as life and twice as natural. You're the lad with the bats in the belfry, aren't you?"

"No, miss," I said, for desperation can make a liar of anybody.

"Get along with you. I seen you at it myself, all dribble and piss like the draper's cat."

At least her contempt was open and honest, unlike the principal and the bursar, both of whom would rather consider I did not exist.

Even the pupils knew, though there was one young girl I came to recognize who smiled shyly whenever she caught sight of me. I clung to those sweet smiles which so restored my confidence. For several days I foolishly believed that she liked me and wanted to be friendly. Then I saw her giggling at me with another girl and I knew that she had smiled only out of pity.

From being an incarcerated invalid, now I was an outcast. I looked back on the days at Giddings's with longing.

My mother protected me as much as she was able, though it was harder here than in the anonymity of rented rooms. Nor had she given up her quest for a miracle, though now we travelled further afield. At considerable expense and amid much secrecy, letting it be known to the bursar that she was taking me to Chas. Blackman's, gentlemen's outfitters, to be measured up for a Norfolk suit, she took me to a doctor specializing in animal gravitation.

He conducted his science in a house on Kew Green and introduced himself as a disciple of Franz Mesmer, having trained in the great Austrian's own practice in Paris and there witnessed many brilliant cures.

He had a great array of apparatus whose purpose, he said, was too scientific to explain to my mother. I was impressed by the huge magnets which lay upon a chenille tablecloth.

After passing his hands over my head, the doctor said, "I can tell at once that there is much active electricity in this brain."

"Electricity?" said my mother uncertainly. "Like the electricity that we are told is present in lightning?"

"Precisely the same."

I did not care for the jagged forks of lightning in a storm any more than for their counterpart in my brain. Both were too bright, too sudden, and capable of causing immense destruction.

"Electricity," the doctor continued, "while it is an interesting natural phenomenon, has a complete lack of any practical use in any of its forms. And when contained within the human skull causes much suffering."

I agreed.

"It must therefore be drawn out. In this form, it is known as animal magnetism and must be harnessed."

My mother, who was seated at one side of the consulting room, gasped as the doctor took up the big magnets which so intrigued me, to pass them over my head and draw out whatever this stuff was.

"Madam, let me assure you at once that this procedure is entirely safe. I am a member of the Electrical Society of London. The great Dr. Franz Mesmer himself, inventor of this exceptional technique, was so skilled he was actually able to dispense with the use of magnets and used his bare hands to draw out the animal gravitation. With his own hands, he also could infuse the corpus with the essential mesmeric fluids of life. However, I prefer to use the technical apparatus, for as we now know, electricity and magnetism are more closely connected than even Dr. Franz realized."

I asked if the removal would hurt.

"It is an invisible fluid, diffusing itself through your system like plasma," he said. "I assure you, you will feel nothing beyond a slight chilliness and some oppression."

The treatment, unlike Mr. Gosforth's, did not induce any increase in seizures. Nor did it inhibit them.

On our next clandestine outing, we went to a haematic specialist in Hammersmith. He made numerous small incisions in my scalp to draw out small quantities of blood.

"Diseased tissue," he explained, "gives off an abnormal amount of energy. These life-force energies can be detected in the blood. By some means, they must be replaced. The diseased tissue of his brain is depleting him. Each time there is a loss of life-force energy, he suffers a fit."

As the blood was withdrawn from my scalp, my mother fainted and had to be revived by the haematologist's assistant with a saucer of burning feathers under her nose.

We did not persevere with the specialist from Hammersmith, and I took refuge in the school kitchens, where the cook, for reasons of her own, had taken an interest in my welfare.

"You mustn't mind what the others say, duckie. But you know how it is. They've all of them seen you taking one of your poorly turns. And it's not a pretty sight, though you'd be the last to know it, wouldn't you, dearie?"

"I'm sorry," I mumbled. I was truly ashamed. The image of the thrashing woman on the towpath at Hampton Court lingered with me.

"You won't change their way of thinking. That's the way it is. Just keep out of their way if you can, that's my advice. Here, look, I've got something for you. There was this wee bitty over from my pastry. So I've baked you a currant twist. Mind now, it's hot."

Another time, she bluntly informed me, "Had a nephew like you, died though. Took one turn, real bad, and never came back to us. Why don't you try a teaspoon of salt, common salt, on the back of your tongue, just the minute you feel one of them turns coming on. Sit quiet and I'll read the embers for you."

She went over to the range and gave the embers a good stir with the poker. As the cinders fell through the horizontal bars into the fire-basket, she watched them closely.

"No, you'll not be taking a turn for a day or two," she pronounced. "See the way they've fallen, calm and evenly spread?"

I tried to explain how I sometimes was fortunate enough to get a moment's premonitory warning.

"That's all fine and good, but you have to find the pattern to them. You find the pattern to your convulsions and you'll be right as rain."

I was keeping up my diary, marking each seizure of which I was aware, and still no pattern had emerged.

She said she'd keep a firm eye on the ashes of the fire for me. "And meanwhile, a nice cup of camomile, that's what you need. Soothing and sedative to all parts. You're a highly strung laddie, that's your trouble. And no wonder with the sad time of it you've had, not to mention your poor ma."

But another day she changed the recipe. "Mistletoe," she told me when I was confined to bed with a cracked rib. "And pennyroyal. Those are the two you need."

She made me various infusions of leaves and herbs, changing the variety according to some undisclosed system. I drank them, once the rib was less painful, sitting on a little three-legged stool by her range watching out for the fall of the cinders to report to the cook whether they were short or elongated, sparkling or dull.

"And your mother could do with a peppermint brew from the look of her. Very peaky, poor dear. But peppermint, that always does the trick with vomiting."

The Academy did not employ its own washerwoman but had one in from the village weekly. She was a Cornishwoman and she, too, added her pennyworth of opinion. She believed in dowsing.

"Striking with the dowsing-rod, that's what he needs," she told the cook. "Drive out those devils in him."

"Nonsense," said the cook. "That sort of talk is nothing but old-fashioned nonsense." And she advised me to keep away from the kitchen on Mondays.

With the devils, and the evil, and the animal gravitation forces, my highly strung brain was a busy place. I welcomed the attention of the old women, but their interest did little good. The convulsions were mine alone and could not be shared. When I went into the deep and cavernous place of the fit, I had to depart and return entirely on my own.

Eight

The bursar had a set of rooms within the school into which my mother moved. I was initially given a lumber room tucked away in the attic, where I would have preferred to remain. But the principal soon had me moved down to the bursar's dressing-room so that, in the eventuality of a disaster, my mother would be on hand.

In that small anteroom I could hear everything that went on between them.

Frequently, there was arguing, to which I was forced to listen even though I put two feather pillows over my head.

"Don't you see, my dear, how he is finding it ever more degrading, more humiliating, as you force him through these ridiculous charades? You will betray any courage or dignity which the poor boy has left."

I heard her reply. "It was a certified hypnotist of the highest repute. We saw his diplomas, framed, and signed, displayed on the walls of his consulting room."

"Hypnotism, my dear, is merely a state of abnormal suggestibility, no more than that. I am wiser than you, more experienced in all matters of the world. And I *know* these things."

"How *can* you know?"

"I know that there are some situations in life which one must accept."

"I won't, I won't accept it," she sobbed.

"And one must carry out a dignified battle against hysterical despair."

How easy it must be, I thought, for him to speak with such sensible detachment when it was not he, but she, who carried the curse of having me, she who cared for me so much that she had married this man for my benefit, so that I might have a secure roof over my head, and three full meals a day brought up to my room.

Perhaps her sacrifice was too much. Her crying voice became almost inaudible. "He is *my* son. You don't know how it is."

"Calm yourself, my dear."

"Oh, oh, oh."

"Forgive me for speaking so frankly, but it has to be said. You have allowed yourself to be made an emotional slave to every one of these foolish quacks who can only offer false hopes. You are encouraging the boy to accept superstitious practices. You are not relieving his suffering but prolonging it. From now on, this miracle-seeking must stop."

The following day, while my mother was with pupils in the music room, the bursar called me down to his office. He asked me if I was feeling all right. I said that I was. I did not tell him I was lonely and unhappy. He asked me to sit down. I did so.

"Albert, there is an important topic I have to tell you about."

"I have changed my name to Edward, sir."

"Very well, Edward. The matter concerns your welfare. Mrs. Bittern and I have very different ideas about illness and their causes, and about the best manner of their management. I am unable to accept any of the magical notions with which you and she have been experimenting. Do you understand what I am talking about?"

"I believe so."

"We are all of us likely to be subjected to various kinds of suffering at various times. Such is life. Whether we live long, or whether we die early, is to some extent immaterial. For at the end, all of us die. However, during our time on earth, it is the responsibility of those in sound health, like myself, to ensure that weaker persons, like yourself, do not suffer unnecessarily. As your stepfather, and as a man with a far greater knowledge of the world than Mrs. Bittern, I am not prepared to stand by and watch you being put under the constant emotional pressure to follow all these ridiculous antics week by week, quite aside from the financial cost."

The infusions of pimpernel, mistletoe, or skullcap, prepared by the cook, and the beatings by the Cornishwoman with her mystic rod, had cost him nothing.

"You must never again allow yourself to be blackmailed into doing these nonsensical things. You must not weakly capitulate to futile hopes for unlikely and impossible cures. The servants are employed to work here, not to deliver potions to you, and these other people you have been seeing are charlatans, and shamans, witch doctors, and imposters. There is no science in what they claim to do, only irresponsible charade. I am a free thinker and I do not hold with popery or quackery. Do you understand?"

"Yes, sir." I bowed my head in the shame of knowing that my mother had been so easily duped. I believed him. But how could I allow such disloyalty to her by admitting that she was wrong and he was right?

"From now on, all miracle-seeking is to cease. And should Mrs. Bittern attempt any more, you are to come and inform me."

Did he believe I would commit such treachery? Besides, my mother was seeing less of me. She was so fully occupied with her teaching duties and with the holy state of matrimony that she seemed to have lost interest in my well-being.

I was now more solitary than I would have thought it possible to be. My life was either alone in the cramped dressing-room or taking secret teas with the cook in the kitchen. And in between were the days of blackness, which, according to the inky crosses in my diary, were occurring at approximately twenty episodes a month.

Alone in my room, I caught the convivial sounds of others at work, study, or recreation, which only served to heighten my own self-pity. There was the cheerful chatter of the maids drifting up from the servants' quarters, the chanting of pupils from the classroom, the scrape of their bows on strings from the music room, and the wooden click and outdoor laughter of pupils playing croquet or French cricket on the lawns.

Even the animal kingdom had companionship. The cows stood chewing in thoughtful groups, or waded in their friendly line into the water in search of greener clumps of verdure. The swifts flew screaming through the air in summer packs, and all the while I was obliged to skulk in dim corners. Watching the slow-moving cows, I thought of Lawrie, waking each morning to another day of drudgery as bondsman to Giddings, borne up by the image of his holy man grilling on the fire. I had not even a patron saint to whom I could pray.

All day, I had nothing to do. I missed even the company of the painted flowers on which I had once had to work so hard. I remembered a set of twelve which had been for a special issue entitled *The Language of Flowers*. How thrilled my mother had been to be asked by Mr. Dukes, not for a single illustration, but for a whole dozen at one time.

I remembered her explaining to me the virtues of each flower to be represented.

"Convolvulus stands for humility. The forget-me-not is for true joy. Pansy for thought. Cowslip for winning grace."

Even now, I could complete the recitation as though it were a poem.

"China aster for mutual love. Bluebell for constancy." These were such strange values on which to build a life. Could any lady, receiving as a gift *The Language of Flowers*, hope to achieve them all?

There was no flower, or none that I could recall, for humour, nor for bravery in the face of desolation. However, given that I had no patron saint, I knew which flower should have been my emblem. The clematis was the flower for mental health. It was a simple plant, with an attractive if insignificant blossom. It grew twisting and turning, tall and straggly, turning round and round this way and that, desperately in need of supports to hold it up, unable to cling strongly as the sweet pea or the convolvulus manage to do. It required its roots to be kept dark and shady, yet its upper parts were always reaching up for the light. It was vulnerable to death if neglected. Mr. Dukes had decided to omit the clematis from *The Language of Flowers*.

The dressing-room was a narrow room with panelled walls, a tall panelled door, and a tall sash window at the far end. It was painted light grey. There was room for the single bed alongside the wall, the washstand, and the firegrate, which never contained the warmth of a lighted fire.

Late one afternoon when I was creeping invisibly through the shadows of the Academy, I took some paper from an empty classroom and hid it beneath the mattress in my room. Now, during the empty days when I had nothing to do but stand at the sash window or sit on the bed, I could draw the room around me.

On the first of many attempts, the perspective was wrong, as was the way the light entered and fell against the panelling. But I achieved, eventually, a fine clear line drawing where perspective and shading were right, in which the panelled walls looked as they were, in which the shading was as it was. It was a clean, clear, empty room, for I, the draughtsman, could not be seen.

I was satisfied with my achievement. I mounted the finished drawing on card, and on my mother's birthday, I left it in her room. But she never mentioned it.

The bursar and she continued to have numerous disputes in which, sadly, I was usually the topic. She never spoke to me of these differences.

For so long, she had run her own life. Much as she had wanted a man to care for her, take responsibility from her, in reality it was proving tiresome to accept his authority.

On some occasions I heard her end a discussion in a sultry silence.

On another, their door opened and closed and I heard her rush away down the corridor. I opened my own door to see if I could offer some kind of filial comfort. I saw her stuffing her hands to her mouth as though to prevent herself from shouting aloud in frustration.

"Mother?" I whispered.

But she did not or would not hear me and scuttled back into their rooms still with her hands pressed up to her mouth, after which I heard him speak more gently.

Another day, I heard him ask why she did not wear the turquoise and crystallite brooch that he had given her at their marriage. She did not reply. He asked again what had become of it. He must have known that she had sold it, for I heard him say, "I have told you, you must not continue to allow yourself to be duped by these foolish people. They can only offer false hopes."

"One more," she implored him. "Just one more. I beseech you. The water cure is not quackery. It is practised by qualified physicians from London's teaching hospitals. All I need is the fare to send him to Margate. Please, please let me try this one last one."

"Enough! The matter is closed."

Outside their rooms, they never raised their voices or gave any indication of discord. Their demeanour was always fitting for an Academy of Learning. But I could tell when an argument had taken place by the stiff, doll-like way my mother processed down to the dining-room for the Morning Prayers from which I was excluded. They walked side by side, as a devoted couple, yet inches apart so that not even their clothes should touch.

But I discovered that they had their times of contentment, too. Once, when staring from my window on a still balmy evening, I caught sight of them walking the gravel path from the French windows, down to the riverbank, not touching but very close. As the red-warblers chortled and gurgled a twilight song, I watched Mr. and Mrs. Bittern disappear into the hanging mist, and they seemed like two fairy-tale characters, entirely cloaked in a private enchantment.

It was from the cook that I learned my mother was with child.

I found this information impossible to believe or accept.

Nine

"You are lying and I shall not listen!" I said. "Mr. Bittern warned me I would hear only superstitious gossip from your sort. You're just an ignorant servant."

My body began to quiver, not with the onset of a seizure, but with the spasms of a terrible anger.

Why should this being have the future benefit of a father when I had not?

When I reconsidered the question, I knew the answer and the trembling ceased. Anger was a luxury I did not deserve.

I was owed nothing, for I was a degenerate defective who was already in receipt of far more than was my due, being fed and clothed through the goodwill of Mr. Bittern.

But he did not give me affection. And even such interest as I had once had from my mother, he now claimed for himself. With his grey coldness, was it possible to think of him as a suitable parent for a child?

Perhaps he would change and become gentle and caring,

as I had fleetingly seen him be with his wife on those quiet evenings scented with moss and yellow flag irises, when they were alone, or thought they were alone, disturbed only by the peeping of a moorhen in the reeds.

The gossiping servants said he would change with fatherhood.

"Seen it a thousand times. A hard man becomes soft when there's a baby in the crib."

The cook said that he had changed already. "That woman, even if she did emerge from God knows where, hasn't she already done him the power of good?"

My mother, the mother of this other child, swelled and swelled till she could scarcely walk, not only her belly but also her feet, her hands, and her face. The cook told me it was because of her age she was unable to excrete water from her body.

The child arrived before its time but in fine health. My mother's health deteriorated. She developed pneumonia. Her breathing sounded like the gurgling of a brook in spring, for her infected lungs were filling with fluid.

When she could no longer sit upright without help, she must have known that she would never get out of her bed again. She roused herself enough to ask for a priest to be called in to hear her confession.

Mr. Bittern did not approve of priests or confessions, but to humour her he sent for the rector who had married them.

This was one of the grand moments of her life, far greater than her discreet and hurried marriage. She was the centrepiece. Her hair was fluffed up, with a newly starched white cap on top. She wore a voluminous ruffled nightgown with a pink silk jacket over it, and the room was scented with burned rosemary stems to counter the odour of sickness.

"If only I could cross over the river to die in Richmond," she confided in me in gurgling gasps.

"You are not dying, Mother," I said. "They say you are past the crisis and will soon be regaining strength."

"Like Henry. And Edward. And Elizabeth. Ah, now Elizabeth, and that would be most singular, to pass away upright upon my throne within sound of the clattering hoofs."

"Clattering hoofs?" I said, wondering if she was delirious again.

"The horses, Albert. Do you remember nothing? The queen's messengers. How they waited at Richmond palace beneath her majesty's window to take the news north as soon as she died. What a moment of royal glory."

The rector arrived, not robed in white as at the marriage, but in his dull black suit with bread crumbs in his moustache.

Waiting outside her room, I thought how there was no real wickedness in her, so she could not have much to confess apart from her exaggerated penchant for royalty.

When the rector had done his business, I returned to her room.

She was lying back exhausted, her neat little cap all crooked on her head, and I sensed that the acting was over.

The rector had left her a little card printed in decorative script with a message for the dying. *Lord, I may be busy this day. If I forget thee, do not thou forget me.* He had left it tucked, like a playing card, in her clasped hands. She was too weak to let it go.

"Get rid of this, rid of it." Her irritable words came up her windpipe in short spluttering bursts. Once I had removed the card from her hands, she seemed to become more relaxed.

Over the next two days her mind flowed in and out of consciousness. I sat by her whenever I could slip into the room unnoticed. I knew that she was dying when the cook sent me up an extra piece of gingercake on my supper tray.

Mr. Bittern seemed still unbelieving that Mrs. Bittern was to leave him. He strode efficiently about, up and down the stairs, in and out of the room, calling for more coal for the fire, more air for her to breathe, more poultices, more broth, less noise, less air, less commotion.

In the early afternoon, while I chanced to be alone in the room, she swam up into one of her periods of lucidity. I was beside the bed, staring absently from the window at the leaves outside being turned upwards by the wind to reveal their pale underside sadness. I thought she was sleeping so was startled to feel the clammy hand take mine. She whispered that she was going to make her last confession.

"But, Mother dearest, you have already done that to the Reverend Pritchard."

"Bah, bah, bah!" she said.

Was she raving?

"That one. Just for show. Now listen well, Albert Edward. I have done as much for you as I could. And it was not enough. Now you will have to manage on your own."

"Mother."

"You were always doomed to live. You were created with such passion, so much true love. I tried to care for you as if you were a normal child. Now I see it would have been better if you had died at the start. You don't know the burden of it, to cart around a peculiarity. You will always be a queer stranger in this world."

I withdrew my hand angrily from hers. "Then why did you love me?"

She did not or could not answer. Perhaps she had never loved me.

In a voice so small I could hardly hear, she said, "Take care of him, please."

It was unclear if she referred to the baby child or to Mr. Bittern.

I left her room and went back to my own. Why should she die and I, the burden, continue to live?

She passed away later that evening, by which time I was quite dried out of tears.

I did not attend the burial although I prepared for it. Upon my bed, a black tie and a black crepe armband had been laid out for me to wear.

I went over to the looking glass with the tie so that I would knot it neatly. I tasted an unpleasant taste in my mouth and I heard a peculiar ringing in my ears. I felt terribly weak and wanted to sit down. I thought it was emotion for my mother, for all morning I had been feeling wretched and as though I were on the brink of breaking down in tears.

As I glanced at the reflection of the black tie, half-tied around my neck and my hands fumbling with it, I felt a numbness in my left arm, and it would not do what it should. I had to hurry to be ready for the funeral, but the arm would not cooperate in tying the tie which would show my mourning. Then my whole left side became numb. I saw my face in the glass and the left side appeared to have dropped so that my mouth hung open like Lawrie's.

"Oh no! Not now!" I cried to myself. "It is one of those things coming on me." But I could not remember what the things were and what they were called. I knew only that one of them was starting.

Sure enough, the bedroom carpet began to heave up towards me, the ceiling began to press down with its doom-laden prophecy, and the panic set in. But the thing that was coming to me seemed to take a long time.

Like my mother's dying, when there can only have been seconds between her being alive and breathing, and her being functionless and dead, there can only have been seconds between my being aware and being unaware. Yet it seemed to last an eternity. Those few seconds were the worst seconds because I knew where I was going and there was nothing I could do. At last, I felt myself falling towards the floor as the twitching in my body began. And then I was pulled down into the blackness.

When I came back to the world, I was confused. The room was different.

It had been cleared of every breakable object, including the lamp with its glass shade, so that it was now more like a hermit's cell. As I later discovered, this was on the orders of the principal. There remained a bed and bedcovers, but nothing more. Even the white china chamber beneath the bed had been removed lest I fall upon it and injure myself. If I needed, in the night, to relieve myself, was I to use the window or the fire-grate?

When my head began to clear and I remembered who

and where I was, I recalled that she had said, "Take care of him, Albert."

She had meant her baby. But he was no longer there. There were no signs of any baby having been there.

The cook told me he had been sent to a woman in Ham.

I went to the bursar to ask why the child had been given away.

In his grief, he seemed to have forgotten my existence, rather as I would have liked to have forgotten his, for he focused blankly on my face and stared right through me as though he had no idea who I was.

"The child has gone to a wet nurse. And that's where he will stay. And what business is it of yours?"

"No business, sir. I ask out of personal interest, since the baby was Mrs. Bittern's younger son and I am her elder one."

"You are not my son. I have no son like you."

"No, sir. I make no claim to that. I am your wife's son."

"I have no wife." He looked at me hard, then opened his mouth and began to wail with a sound like a hundred damp sheep bleating. "Whoever you are, I can't bear the sight of you. So go, go!"

So I went, quickly, because I was afraid he wanted to hit me. But where was I to go? I had nowhere. I had not even a wet nurse in Ham. I fled from his office, out of the hall, through the gardens, and toward the river. When I reached the bank, I stumbled along it.

I walked for what felt like miles but there was no path, and with the briars and slashing stems, I made a slow progress. I was trying to make my way downstream to the only friend in the world I had. Long before I reached any area that remotely resembled Mortlake, the terrain disintegrated into unfamiliar swampy pools harbouring the rotting hulks of drowned barges, and a riverbank composed of slimy and decaying earth. I passed hovels where strange rodentlike families dwelt in squalor and grey-skinned children played in muddy creeks. They did not answer me when I asked them where the ferry crossing was and if Water Lane was near.

Perhaps I had walked so far that I had passed by Mortlake. Perhaps I was now nearly in London. The river seemed to have grown wider, more like a lake.

As it grew dark, I was lost and afraid. A strong wind blew across the river and the water turned black. The only sound was the wind in the scrubby bushes.

If I could reach Lawrie, he would take me in.

I saw tiny lights on the far bank which might have been the warehouses of Water Lane.

I shouted towards the tiny lights, "Ferry man! Ferry man!"

There was no answering call and no splash of the boatman coming over to pick me up.

I called out for Lawrie, shouting his name again and again and again into the blackness of the river. "Lawrie, Lawrie, Lawrie. It's brother Edward, come and help me. Please!" The wind just blew my voice back at me.

But something on this side heard and was coming for me, crashing through the vegetation, wading through the mud. I did not know if it was an escaped zoological creature on the rampage, or a criminal, or a body-snatcher, or, as I had read of in *The Illustrated London News*, a scalp-hunter sent out by the wig-makers of Holborn in search of human hair. I knew only that my heart was pounding with terror.

The light of a lantern was bounding jerkily nearer and I heard panting. The approaching menace was human.

I crouched down low amongst the dank-smelling vegetation.

The lantern light stopped. The dangerous breathing of the man was just behind me.

"Forgive me. Forgive me."

I saw nothing.

"Forgive me. I should not have said what I did. It was because you look too much like your mother."

I crawled out from beneath the leaves and revealed my face in the light.

"I did not consider what I was doing. Forgive me, I beg you."

"Yes, sir," I said.

"Say it. Please say it."

"I forgive you," I said, though I had not much idea what it was about. Was he to be forgiven for weeping and openly showing his grief?

"Thank you." The bursar held out his hand. I took it. We shook hands briefly but formally and then, by the light of his lantern, we made our way back the way we had both come. He spoke once more.

"You must not walk alone by the river again. It is too dangerous for you. You could drown."

By morning, he had regained his composure and was as stiff and upright as ever.

He had not chosen me for his life's companion any more

than I had chosen him. We had been forced by fate into each other's lives, and now we had each of us lost the person we really loved. Yet this did not offer any sense of unity. Indeed it divided us further. We had each cared for her in such different ways.

If I had been more sensitive to his pain, I might have seen that his grief, his loss, was greater than my own. But he did not again let any emotion show.

He was, as he reminded me, a rational thinker.

He directed all the energy of his grieving towards finding an explanation for the sharp increase in my convulsive disorder.

I was growing away from my boyhood. I was at the watershed between being a child and becoming a man. With these changes, so the incidents were increasing, not one a month, nor one in seven days. And the seizures were not only more frequent, but more erratically so and lasting longer, so the days merged with nights, nights with days. No sooner did I find myself gratefully recovering from one than the subsequent had devoured me.

"I have been driven by despair at your suffering to investigate your malady in a methodical manner. And it would appear that my original surmise was correct. There is no known clinical treatment that has yet proved effective. However, there are sensible remedies we can undertake. A careful diet, keeping the bowels well open, and plenty of exercise are thought to be beneficial. It is certainly true that you have been spending much time alone in your room."

He ordained his regime of daily walking, up and down the grounds, come rain or shine. And the episodes of my departure from the world continued as before. Mr. Bittern kept his own record, though his was less accurate than my own black crosses in the diary, for he also counted it a fit if I stayed in my room brooding.

After a full trial of the walking regime, Mr. Bittern recalled me to his office, his disappointment as great as my own. However, he had an important new area of management to discuss, though it was one which he found difficult to broach.

"There is a provoker of fits we have not mentioned before," he said, looking away at the wall behind me rather than into my face. "Concerning your·personal conduct. It would seem from the increasing frequency in my record book that this could be an important area for our attention. You are old enough to understand what I am referring to?"

I wasn't sure.

"I mean, have you been playing with yourself in any way that you should not? There are parts of your person which should not be handled for your own pleasure."

My mother had made one reference to this. When I was very young and waking from a fit, she had warned me that, "The demon comes to little boys who play with themselves."

Mr. Bittern said, "You must maintain restraint and personal discipline *at all times*, and especially when you are alone. I do know what I am talking about, for I, too, have been a vigorous young man with all the natural desires of the flesh. Self-abuse is no habit for any man to get into. For those of your disposition, it is exceedingly dangerous."

If only I could have found solace so easily. In fact, when alone in my room, I spent far more of my time habouring morbid thoughts of death.

"It is an established fact that acts of self-comfort have a direct effect on the brain, which in turn leads to an increased tendency to fits. As you know, epilepsy leads to pronounced deterioration of the brain and eventually to death."

"But, sir, as you yourself said, we are all of us destined to die sooner or later. So does it really matter?" I was inclined to wish it to be sooner and had begun to consider the various available methods of achieving extinction. Mr. Bittern admonished me severely. Thoughts of self-destruction were nearly as bad as acts of self-gratification.

To control the latter, he had made for me a simple harness of soft leather which was fitted under the mattress, with the wrist-loops secured over the top of the bedcovers.

"At night, before you lie down, you fasten these small restrainers to each wrist which will secure your hands so even when you sleep they will lie beside you. Then there will be no danger of them roaming about your body to do you mischief."

I did as he told me. The harness was not seriously uncomfortable. However, it prevented one from being able to turn over, ensuring that one slept on one's back all night. Whether it successfully inhibited acts of self-gratification while I slept, and whether Mr. Bittern crept in to check on me in the night, I had no idea.

I only knew that one fine day the paper and sketches

which I kept hidden beneath the mattress were gone, as was the harness, which was not mentioned again.

He had a new plan. He was getting rid of me.

"I have been investigating further into your malady. As a last resort, I am sending you to Margate for the water cure, just as your mother would have wished."

Ten

Margate, the bursar explained, was a coastal fishing port in the county of Kent, situated at the mouth of the Thames estuary.

"It is a considerable distance, but you will be well cared for, and I have been reliably informed of the therapeutic value of sea water and sea air. I have written to the Chief Medical Superintendent to notify him of your arrival."

The simplest, if not the speediest, method of transporting me was to send me on one of the pleasure boats which zig-zagged back and forth, also up and down, right to the heart of London. There, I would board a larger coastal vessel to take me the rest of the way.

The under-gardener, a strapping young man with earthy fingers, was chosen to escort me on the first stage as he was felt to be strong enough to restrain me if it became necessary.

We travelled third class at a cost of one shilling, four pence for his return ticket, and ten pence for mine, which was one-way only. The bursar paid.

The under-gardener was at first wary that I might at any moment cause a disturbance, or attract attention, or throw myself overboard. I tried to put him at his ease and when, some short distance into our journey near Chiswick Reach, he realized that I was not intent on causing him trouble, he quite bucked up and was even prepared to answer when I spoke to him.

I had a flask of cold tea and some fresh bread, mutton, and pickle, prepared for me by the cook. He had nothing. On reaching Putney Wharves, he had relaxed enough to share my meal, so I asked if we might sit, not below in the stuffy saloon where the bursar had placed us, but on the upper forward deck near the bow.

We passed much river traffic, including cargo vessels, slow-moving dredgers, and sailing barges so heavily laden it seemed they would sink when the next wash of water slurped onto them.

I had little idea where I was being sent, yet I felt relief to be leaving behind the stifling sadness of that place of my mother's death. Indeed, the further we travelled, the more my spirits lifted. Never before had I been allowed on such a magnificent adventure. I imagined myself an explorer, setting out into the great world. The wide choppy water before me was Plymouth Sound and I Sir Walter Raleigh off to discover the excitement of the potato tuber and the *Nicotiana*. Then the swirling flow before me became the massive River Niger as we steamed through the mangrove swamps and palm groves of black Africa.

My custodian had never been so far from home either, though he knew, by repute, many of the landmarks that we passed.

The river snaked and curved its way past churches and abbeys, piers and jetties, palaces and bridges and innumerable wharfs, Plantation, Lensury, Regents, Chelsea, and Trinidad, where exotic goods from halfway across the world and beyond were being landed.

Close after the Tower of London we came to the Pool of London. This was filled with shipping departing for and arriving from all across the globe, so many maritime vessels, schooners, and brigs, barques, and cutters, that their masts and rigging appeared as giant spiders' webs against the sky.

Here I was to board one of the Margate hoys which regularly carried their human cargo of day-trippers down the coast. The under-gardener purchased my ticket, one-way only. He was then to hand me over into the care of a responsible individual. But since there was nobody about who was not thoroughly occupied, either with the important enjoyment of a sea-outing, or with manning the ship, he merely patted me on the shoulder, thanked me for the mutton, and hurriedly left me.

Thus, unhampered by supervision, I was free to enjoy the second stage of the trip as much as the first. A large family settled itself and its picnic baskets on an upturned rescue raft nearby, and the mother urged me to join them.

"Come on, dearie. Sitting's as cheap as standing. Plenty of space for a little one on here." They all moved up to make room for me, which enabled me to eavesdrop on the father's cheerful commentary of the passing scene.

After Woolwich, Creekmouth, Purfleet, and Grays had all been pointed out, the river made its last great curve at Standford-le-Hope, and then, with land receding from us on either side, we were out at sea. Overhead was an open sky, and screaming gulls followed in our wake. I admired the skill of the pilot, who, despite the speed we put on as the sails filled out, avoided collision with small fishing craft, sandflats, and the wooden posts of the oyster beds.

Ahead of us, upon the desolate windswept land, was a tall crumbling tower which I supposed, in my ignorance, to be the lighthouse of Margate, but was quickly corrected by the father in the party beside me.

"Reculver, laddie. Roman fortress they left behind when they fled. Quite a landmark for sailors in winter, that is."

He pointed out to me that the harbour of Margate was just beyond, with its windmills on the hill above all turning merrily in the breeze.

As our boat was changing course, there was a scurry of activity as passengers rushed to one side to peer out across the waves. I joined them and was almost beside myself with delight.

Twenty miles distant, quivering in the blur between sea and sky, hung a narrow ribbon of coastline.

Never had I expected the trip to bring such a thrill and I felt as though I would not mind what might happen to me next. I was looking at a foreign country. Even my mother, who spoke the language of the French, had never set eyes on France as I now had.

A reputation for violence and uncontrollability had evidently travelled ahead of me, no doubt via the bursar's letter, for I was met off the hoy by two male medical orderlies, equipped with a bentwood and cane spinal-chair in case I could not walk and a canvas straitjacket in case I was in need of restraining.

But they were friendly fellows and seemed pleasantly relieved to discover that I travelled alone and had the use of two good legs. So they decided to drop in at The Nag's Head and stand me a jar of small beer. I had never before entered a public house and I greatly enjoyed it. The atmosphere was convivial and the customers in holiday mood. Through the open door of the bar, I saw how the colours, even of such everyday things as tiled rooftops and sails in the breeze, were brighter here. I wished I had thought to bring my mother's water paints so that I might try to capture all these new visual delights.

My guardians struck up a conversation with every person who entered. By the time they were into their seventh pints of ale and no longer standing firmly, I deduced it was time for me to set off again on my own.

The spinal-chair was still outside where they had left it. I placed my luggage on the seat and, by asking directions a few times, made my way to the hospital. I had great faith in the authenticity of the cure I was to receive. Already, after only an hour in Margate, I was stronger and fitter than I had been for some time, no doubt due to the air, whose briny freshness I could taste and smell.

My destination was easy to find, being an impressively large building sited almost on the shore. Its name and function were carved into the stone wall, *The Royal Sea Bathing Hospital for Sick and Crippled Children.*

How proud my mother would have been to know that I was to benefit from the patronage of royalty.

The porter at the main door questioned me through a

metal grille before he would admit me. As he asked my name, a discordant sound began whining in my ears. I saw him waiting for my answer.

"Your name, lad, just your name. Can't let you in without a name."

I was unable to speak. I opened my mouth intending to explain that I was suddenly unwell and needed to sit. But I could not reach him. Coherent speech would not come out.

I became mesmerized by the action of his lips moving as he spoke again. Although I could hear his words, I could make no sense of them. It was as though he was speaking a foreign language.

I knew where I was, and yet at the same time I did not. I kept thinking again and again, Where am I? What day is it? What am I doing here?

I felt so terribly ill and afraid. I wondered if I was going to die in this strange place where nobody would know who I was or from where I had come. All thoughts in my brain were jumbled into nonsense. I kept thinking of my watercolours and wishing I had painted a picture of myself beside the river at Isleworth so they might know who I was.

Then I dropped down the endless well where there was no time and where I swam in a subfluvial world of fishes and effluent.

And so it was that my arrival and first days at Margate were blurred and distorted by a rapid succession of seizures, one following another. But eventually my brain and my body settled and I could take stock of the situation.

The other inmates were aged from three years up to fourteen and all manner of extraordinary deformities were represented. There were victims of rheumatic fever and the wasting disease, children with unseeing eyes, twisted backs, withered limbs or club feet, such unnaturally misshapen creatures they seemed scarcely children, more like the gargoyles spouting from some ancient church guttering.

We were all of us members of the unfortunate classes, that is, paupers, illegitimates, orphans, and the generally dispossessed. We were also all valiant survivors. Had we not been, then none of us would have lasted this long in a world that had so little room for us.

Hearing others tell of the backgrounds from which they came, I was relieved to have no living natural parents else I might have been found out to be a cheat, an imposter, and a fraud, for my manner of speaking had been acquired through the genteel speech of my mother, and my clothing was that of the son of an academy bursar.

We slept in dormitories with rows of twenty beds down one side, facing twenty more on the other. Having spent my life alone, it was strange to be with others every hour of every day. But quickly I learned to appreciate the chatter and companionship, and since this was not a fever hospital, we were mostly in comparatively good health and high spirits.

When I emerged from the first debilitating week, I noticed how the four legs of every bed in the dormitory stood in a little tin pan of water. This I assumed to be a part of our mysterious water treatment.

Those boys with palsy tended to stick together in a band as though the inadequacy of their bodies would be less if they were united. One of them, with a severe paralysis of the lower limbs, looked at me incredulously. "You weak in the top storey or just an ignorant toff? Them's no cure! Them's to stop you getting nits, innit!"

With so many of us living close together, there were constant outbreaks of head and body lice. The pans of water were to provide an uncrossable moat for the prevention of the spread of vermin.

"They crawl, don't they?" said one of the palsy boys. "Invisible, so you can't see them, in the dead of night, along the floor and up the bed legs. Then you catch them. But they can't swim."

"Like us. We can crawl but we can't swim neither."

"So maybe as how *we're* nits?" They all roared with laughter.

Another of the gang said, "Perhaps he's such a stuck-up dandiprat he don't even know what nits is, innit!"

"Or may be he's too hoity-toity ever to get bit!"

And they all laughed again at their wit.

The tin pans were an ineffective preventative. Within ten days, I, too, was itching and scratching with lice and had to have my hair shaved. It was not with shame but pride that I wore my newly bald head, for it gained me acceptance into this special group.

We were each given a combination of the same four treatments, namely, immersion in cold water piped into the hospital bath-houses from the sea, immersion in heated sea water, gazing upon sea waves, and breathing sea air, though the reasoning behind the treatment differed for each case. For the tubercular child, it was breathing the ozone-laden air which provided the curative effect. For the child with the angry skin disorder, soaking in one of the huge vats of warmed water was prescribed as the balm which would ease her inflamed eruptions. In my own instance, it was total immersion in cold water which was going to cause the necessary shock to my system to jolt it out of its irregular pattern.

I subjected myself unprotestingly. I had to believe that it would work.

We were all taken out to benefit from the air. Some of us walked, some hobbled, and a few were conveyed on litters on spinal carriages with gabardine covers in case of sudden rain. We were an unwieldy-looking group.

The town was known to locals, not as Margate, but as Bartholomew-Fair-by-the-Sea because of the huge numbers of cockneys and other Londoners from roundabout Saint Bow's and Saint Bartholomew's, who were shipped in each Sunday for their breezy day's holiday.

The visiting clientele were not fashionable, and some were downright rude, staring and pointing as though we were yet another local spectacle to be viewed, along with the fishing fleet, the pier, and the turning windmills.

The palsy boys always shouted back at gawpers.

"Had your penn'orth or do you want a ha'penny change?"

A woman within our hearing said to one of our attendants, "Poor little beggars oughtn't to be allowed to live, did they?"

But most got on with their own enjoyment and some were adventurous enough even to take to the sea bathing, though for recreational rather than medical reasons.

We inmates of the Royal Sea Bathing Hospital for Cripples much enjoyed the entertaining spectacle of the bathing machines, and their lovely occupants, in operation. The Margate bathing machine, invented in that town by a kindly Quaker, was not so much a machine as an enclosed carriage on wheels with front door and wooden steps facing seawards, and which, having been hauled by a patient horse down the shingle and right out into the waves, enabled a lady to discreetly enter the water unseen by those on land.

Although she might venture unseen, she was not unnoticed, and we, the hopeless cripples lined up in our orderly group inhaling deeply, laughed and cheered and guffawed at what we imagined was her partially clothed emergence on the far side of her bathing machine and descent into the chilly waves.

We were visited weekly by the chief Medical Superintendent, who reviewed our condition, advising either more or less exposure to sea water and sea air.

After my examination, he explained to the hospital staff, "The classical grand mal attack, such as this youth suffers from, may be divided into four distinct stages. One, the onset. Two, the rigid state. Three, the convulsive stage. Four, the stage of recovery. During stages two and three, the main treatment must be to prevent the convulsion from injuring the patient. There is no fear at this stage of him injuring other people, though the relaxing of the sphincter and the contraction of the abdominal musculature may cause incontinence. A wooden gag should be placed between the teeth before they become clenched, to prevent the patient from biting either himself or those who are assisting him. During stage two, and before stage three has been reached, the clothing should be loosened and the head, the arms, and the legs laid firmly on the ground, with pressure continued for the duration."

While I was getting myself dressed and the Medical Superintendent's attention was turned to the next child, I managed to slide some sheets of paper and a pen holder off his desk and under my shirt. Later I managed to persuade one of the orderlies to procure me ink powder and a pen-nib in exchange for a line drawing of himself which he could present to his sweetheart.

There was one other patient, younger than I, who suffered from the falling sickness. By watching her, I deduced what was done to me during periods of absence.

The moment she was heard to give the involuntary cry which marked the start of her fit, attendants abandoned whatever they were doing and rushed over to thrust the wooden peg past her protruding tongue and into her mouth, then to suppress her thrashing body by the superior force of their own. As many as four or five adults would gather round, their knees in her back or lying on her limbs. Only when the movements were over did they release the unhappy girl and allow her to sleep.

Our daily regime, though strict, was not intentionally harsh, and my time at Margate was, in most other ways, a period of much contentment. I might willingly have stayed forever had it been permitted. For the first time in my life I was not the outsider. We were all of us united and enjoyed a wholesome sense of mutual support such as I had never before experienced. There was only one inmate in that whole institution who rejected all attempts at socialization.

His name was Paolo, though the attendants called him Jack.

"Why do you not call him by his real name?" I asked. "Perhaps he would respond more?"

"We could never call him by a dago name."

"Then why does he have such a name in the first place?"

"His father was a dago sailor from Italy, fetched up on these shores."

I had seen the coast of France as a shimmering strip across a milky sea. Was Italy near to France?

"Could be," said the attendant.

My ignorance was a growing frustration. I seemed always to be hovering on the threshold of knowledge, but never admitted to a full learning or understanding of facts of the world.

In the refectory I was assigned a seat beside Jack. He was a good-looking boy with a fine complexion, searchingly intelligent eyes, and a mass of curly hair. Since we were the most alike of the whole group, being of similar age, able-bodied, and neither of us disfigured in any visible way, I thought we might become friendly.

Of all the people at the hospital, it was he, and another patient, who provided me with my greatest benefits. Each helped me in very different ways to come to understand more of myself and my disability.

One day as we waited for our bowls of soup, I asked Jack, "What is it with you?"

He gazed at me, unblinking.

I said, "I'm sorry if it was offensive to ask. I didn't mean to pry, I just wondered what is your affliction, and if you enjoy your stay here?"

There passed no flicker of expression across his bland face. Perhaps he did not wish to be associated with any of the rest of us. So I let him be.

But it was too late. He let out a howl.

"Don't breathe on my soup! Don't breathe on it."

I said, "I am not breathing on your soup. I am happy with my own." It was cabbage soup with barley.

"I cannot eat if people have breathed on it. The woman always breathed on it. Then I couldn't eat it."

"What woman?"

"The soup has been breathed on. I cannot touch it." And he dashed it to the floor, yelping like a dog.

It was a curious quirk, this fear that others might breathe on his food.

The refectory attendants came over to calm him. I attempted to explain about his fear of breath on his food and that I had inadvertently provoked him. But they took no notice and said he must eat.

"He has the temper on him today," one attendant said.

They sat with him for over an hour, trying to help him to consume at least one mouthful of broth, blowing on each spoonful to cool it for him, which only exacerbated the problem.

At the next meal, they had him seated away on a separate bench where there was no danger of anyone upsetting him. He was eating calmly, face to the wall, and seemed not the least put out to be set apart. Indeed, he seemed to have a general disregard for people, never revealing feeling for any other human being, though he was fixated on a number of inanimate objects. The iron railings which enclosed our world, the drains which carried away our used water, and small broken pieces of terra-cotta all claimed his interest. He owned a small fragment from a broken flowerpot.

He would take it from his pocket and gaze wonderingly at its deep orange colour for long periods.

When he mislaid this splinter of treasure, he fell into a rage of distress, banging his head on the floor and biting his fingers till they bled, yet making no attempt to search for it.

When I found it and placed it in his hand, he gave a

blissful smile, though not at me. He smiled at his worthless talisman.

He was no moron, rather, was highly intelligent. He could calculate in seconds, without recourse to any printed church calendar, the paschal full moon and thus the date on which Easter would fall, or had fallen, for every year from 1752 until 2299.

"Eighteen hundred and seventy-three, on what date did Easter fall?" he would demand excitably. "Tell me, tell me. Do you know? Do you?"

And when, inevitably, one did not, he supplied the answer.

"March the twenty-third. Ask me another, ask me. Give me a date."

He was able to give the date of Christian feasts in any year past or future.

"In the year of our Lord one thousand nine hundred and thirty, Septuagesima Sunday will fall upon February the sixteenth. In the year of our Lord one thousand nine hundred and seventy-three, the Sunday after Trinity will fall upon June the twenty-third."

It was as though he had the Gregorian calendar and the complete Table of Movable Feasts engraved permanently in his mind's eye. Centuries of time stretched ahead and behind him.

While I was attempting to form some meaningful bond of communication with Jack, another inmate was trying to befriend me. But since she was confined to a spinal-chair, I was easily able to make my escape. She was a midget and a hunchback, with a harelip which caused a whistling in her speech. This did not inhibit her from constantly trying to attract my attention. Her name was Mary.

"Hey, you! Grand master Edward," she called to me in her sibilant hissing voice.

"Don't call me that."

She was a casualty of creation. The fact that she dared find me attractive repulsed me even more.

Her chief features were two enormous hands with short stumpy fingers and blunt deformed nails and two tiny but penetrating eyes like peering grey pebbles set deep in her head.

"I wish to talk with you, to show you something important."

"I don't wish to see."

"It is to your own advantage. You have nothing to be ashamed of with the falling sickness."

"I have never been ashamed," I lied.

"I have a book here which concerns your ailment and was thinking how you might like to borrow it. It is by the learned Dr. Galen."

"I do not know him," I said.

"Indeed you cannot. It is two millenia since he lived."

Clumsily, her huge dablike hands thrust the book at me.

I opened it and understood nothing. The shapes of the characters printed on the page were unknown to me. I could not read one word. She was showing it to me as a trick to mock my ignorance.

"So you do not read Greek?" she said in surprise. "But I thought you were educated? You speak like an educated boy."

"No."

"Then that is a great oversight."

Defensively, I said, "I was advised not to by my step-father. In my own interests. Intensive study can bring on brain fever in those with my condition, especially studying subjects that are taxing on the brain."

"Greek is not taxing. Greek is an easy language to master and gives access to many interesting books. If only you knew Greek, you could read for yourself what Dr. Galen has to say, how nature herself has the innate power to heal without so much intervention from outside forces. And Hippocrates, too, has written many aphorisms that could benefit you."

Who was this opinionated cripple to tell me about the falling sickness which had not already been told me by some quack or magician?

"Diseases of fashion come and go through time. Yours is one of the least fashionable but most significant. Many great statesmen and even greater artists have suffered from it. And most have survived to continue their work."

"I know of none," I said angrily, and made my escape to take refuge in my companionship with Jack.

Eleven

He had extreme sensitivity to sudden or loud noises, which could startle him into a rage. Even if spoken to in a normal tone it was too loud. But I discovered he could listen to me quite attentively if I conversed in a whisper. Like me, he enjoyed the soothing sound of the waves slapping repetitively upon the shingly shore. During the outings to breathe the air, we would sit together listening, like two companions at a musical evening, and sometimes to amuse him I drew the sailing ships we could see out at sea.

He was so remarkable in appearance that I drew him, too. Even though I admirably caught the bright unblinking gaze of his eyes and the smooth beauty of his complexion, he did not understand that it was a portrait of himself.

When the other children saw my talent with a pen, many of them clamoured to be drawn also. But I could not bring myself to duplicate their many deformities and drew no more portraits, only ships and sea gulls.

If I was the sketcher and Jack the mental calculator, then

Mary was the reader. She collected reading matter like a broody duck collecting down to line a nest. She had books and journals of all types, in all conditions of use and misuse, in a herring-basket beneath her bed in the girls' dormitory. She guarded it as carefully as a duck guarding eggs. Even the attendants did not dare move the herring-basket for fear of incurring Mary's wrath. Although Mary, enraged, could cause little physical injury, the ululating sounds were enough to trigger a seizure in me, as once they did, and send others running from the hall.

Few of the inmates were literate, most having been refused entry into formal schooling. So Mary, in a good humour or on a good day, would read aloud in her sibilant voice to those who wished to sit and listen. Occasionally she read from her Latin books, keeping the children mesmerized by the unknown sounds and by the expression of attention on her own face even though they understood nothing of what they heard. She read, as well, poetry about nature and rivers and bird life and death, which she said was written by a famous lord.

When she discovered that I was among the few who could read, she invited me to borrow from her collection.

I wondered how such a creature as she had managed to become educated, while all formal education had entirely evaded me.

"It was the nuns."

"Nuns?" I said. "You are a Roman? You do not look like one of them."

"I was not born one. But even if I were, I should not complain about it. It was the Sisters of Small Mercy who took me in. Though whether out of pity or some other form of sentimentality I do not know. All were infant-crazy, so deprived of anything small and succulent to love that they were even prepared to love me. They loved me to distraction, which is why I am content and happy, whereas you who have not been loved enough are miserable and self-pitying. And so I began with the Latin for their singing."

"You *sing*?" With her crumpled torso and breathy voice it seemed unlikely.

"I liked to but the sisters would not let me. What they needed me for was to write out their parts. See how my hand is quite steady!" She held out her big hand with its clawlike fingernails for my inspection. "They needed their music copied out. Understanding the Latin made errors less likely."

Besides the Greek and Latin books that Mary had accumulated, she had also stories and poetry and tedious religious tracts, and a tattered atlas of the world, which, of all her collection, excited me most as I followed with my finger the waterways of the world.

There was a curious book of short four-lined verses, each accompanied by a strange spidery drawing. The covers and first pages of the book had been torn away, which was why Mary had been allowed to have it. I read what remained but I did not like it.

It frightened me. The illustrations for each of the verses were of deformed figures with noses which reached to the ground, set on heads that were either too large or too small, with stringy legs or stumpy, dislocated arms, just like many of us here, though with the difference that these gross or pinheaded picture-characters were not hospitalized but were free to live independently and do strange things, baking alive their husbands, walking about on the tips of their toes, falling into basins of soup. There was a midget man, the smallest as ever was born, who was devoured by a puppy. There was a man of Koblenz whose legs were immense, and who suffered terrible dreams, just as I frequently did.

"What does it mean?" I asked Mary.

"It is a children's book."

"What is a children's book?"

"One that has been written expressly for their amusement, not for their education."

The coverless, broken-backed book did not amuse me.

"It makes no sense," I said. "It is all nonsense."

"That is its title, *A Book of Nonsense*. It is intended as nonsense. If you do not care for it, then return it please without criticizing things you do not understand," Mary said. She took it back in her flapping hands which so resembled those of one of the characters in her book, the horrible person of Cheadle who was put in the stocks by the beadle.

"It is not that I do not care for it. I do not understand it," I said.

The man of Dutton whose head was as small as a button haunted me, even after I had returned the book to the herring-basket. Dutton was upriver from Richmond. Lawrie had spoken of it. And many of the verses concerned towns and villages along the Thames whose names I knew.

The person of Putney, downriver from Isleworth, was the one who ate roast spiders and chutney. The one from Barnes wore garments covered with darns. There was a young person of Kew, and a man from Sheen, and an abruptious one from Thames Ditton who called for something to sit on. I wondered by what right this verse-writer mocked misshapen people to whom terrible things happened.

I persisted with my one-sided friendship with Jack.

When I listened to him embark upon his chanting calculations of church feasts, I saw that, however powerful his mathematical brain, he was unable to put it to any use. And when I watched him staring with wonder at his piece of pottery, or listening with awe to the waves on the shore, I saw how he was as innocent as a little child, yet he was not a child because, like me, and Mary, too, he was nearly an adult. And I felt that for him there was no hope.

However, through him I gained something important. I came to recognize that I would infinitely rather be who I was, with my kind of fits that I half understood, than he with his who understood nothing. Of all my companions at Margate, he was the only one who was, in my view, genuinely and completely insane.

"Why do you bother with him?" one the palsy boys once asked me. "He's just a shovelhead. Salt water won't never do him no good."

"I know," I said. "But I like him. He reminds me of another friend I once had."

One afternoon, on our return from the daily expedition to breathe the air, Jack was found to be missing. Everybody recalled having seen him with the group as we set out. I had sat with him for a while, then had been drawn into conversation with Mary, who wished to explain to me Hippocrates's view that all physical and mental ability was dependent upon the four humours of blood, phlegm, yellow bile, and black bile. Nowhere in her dissertation was sin.

Nobody remembered seeing Jack wander away.

Three days later, he was washed up near the Roman fortress at Reculver.

At the inquest, the coroner declared it a clear case of self-destruction, which provided the attendants with the advantage that they were not held responsible, but was a disservice to Jack since, as a suicide, he could not be buried on hallowed ground, nor have any service of the Burial of the Dead said for him.

My own belief was that he had not intentionally taken his life but that he had been lured into the sea by the compelling music of the waves, perhaps with the intention of wanting to walk through the seas to seek the land of his seafaring father.

I grieved for him, and to my surprise was comforted unstintingly by ugly Mary. Perhaps she had been as jealous of my friendship with Jack as I had been of hers with books.

"He won't have gone to heaven, poor little soul," she said. "But he wasn't really a sinner, was he, even if he did lay violent hands upon himself, so he'll have gone to limbo."

"Where is that?"

"Halfway," Mary said. "Not so bad, in limbo, from what I heard from the nuns. Bit like this place really."

She said she would say a Hail Mary for him to make up for him not being buried on holy ground.

Whatever Mary's and Dr. Galen's views on my condition were, they were not entirely the same as those of the Medical Superintendent.

One day, at the conclusion of the weekly examination, he filled in a form and gave it to me to read.

MEDICAL STATEMENT

I have this day examined the above-named patient and hereby certify that the <u>Mental Condition of the Patient is as follows</u>: Fits and seizures. Chronic and incurable.

It is my recommendation to the Hospital Board that the treatment be discontinued. And since the patient's condition does not threaten the Social Order nor cause Social Deviancy, I am also of the opinion that he need not be confined to any asylum and may be safely returned home.

<u>The bodily health and condition of the patient are as follows</u>: He is generally in good health and appears to be of average or above-average intelligence.

I read it through. The doctor said, "Do you understand it?"

"I understand the words, yes, sir. But what does it mean? What will become of me?"

"It means that, currently, you are incurable. We can do no more for you."

"But *why* do I have them?"

He did not know. "It is a great mystery and you have to live with it. And since you are an intelligent boy, keep it under your hat, if you can. But let me tell you, in confidence, there is a ray of hope you can cling to. Every person's life moves in a seven-year cycle. That is, every seven years your body changes. At birth, you started to have these seizures. At seven years old, they became less pronounced. A further seven years on, there is another great change, that is, when you reach fourteen, they may become worse or better. Even now you are possibly on the very cusp of change. And in a further seven years, when you are twenty-one, they could cease altogether. Or, should you marry, they might stop altogether, though in general we advise strongly against marriage."

He shook my hand, wished me well, and called for his next patient. It was the unfortunate girl with the skin eruptions, which were that day glowing like coals of fire.

I was dismissed. My six months at Margate were over.

Mary was highly envious that I was leaving so soon.

"For half a farthing I would come with you," she said. "If ever I were freed from this place, I would run as far as I could and join a travelling circus and cavort with the dancing bears."

"You cannot even walk, so how could you expect to dance?"

"You are right," she said, not at all put out. "Then instead, I would marry the first handsome man who would have me."

"That's all very well for a beautiful girl like you," I said. "But what about me? Where am I to go and what am I to do?"

"Go anywhere. Do anything."

"But I cannot," I wailed. "I have not been cured."

"At least you are free! To use your life in whatever way you want."

She gave me as a parting gift one of her precious books. It was written in a foreign language.

"Italian," said Mary. "By a man called Dante. It is about hell."

"Thank you," I said. "But I do not know Italian."

"Then you will learn," she said. It was like an order, or a prophecy.

I was loathe to leave.

After the freshness of the open Channel coast, the inland river atmosphere was stifling.

My first sight of the Academy was of wet sheets hanging in all the windows. The overwhelming smell was of the disinfectant in which they had all been dipped. The place was deathly quiet, which I took at first to be in contrast with the noisy bustle of the bathing hospital.

But the cook told me there had been a disaster.

"Drowning and disease! The two together, would you believe! Not here, dear. Over there, across the other side. With the nobs." She jerked her elbow towards the window. "More than six hundred dead! Can you beat it?"

She repeated the figure with some relish.

"It was the *Queen of the Thames* went over. Yet not one of them that went overboard drowned. It was the cholera that got them instead. They say the water is that bad! And have they been mourned! Heartily so, I can assure you. Went up to see the procession with my own eyes. Half a mile long from Richmond bridge right up to Saint Mary's. And then they had to build a new graveyard just to accommodate them all. And Mr. Rodgers who has been peacefully keeping his hens in the churchyard these past nine years, had to move the pens to make room."

It seemed difficult to accept all parts of the cook's tale, for there were no pleasure-steamers large enough to take as many as six hundred passengers. However, it was true that there had been outbreaks of disease. As the school was situated so close to the water, many parents, fearful of the consequences, had kept pupils away. Several of the staff, too, had left in haste, with the consequence that the bursar had been allowed to remain and his lack of a wife was, for the present, being generously overlooked by the governors.

"They are ignorant people," said the bursar wearily, "who believe that every disease is waterborne, whereas it is a well-known fact that miasmas and bad airs are frequently as much to blame."

The dipped sheets were to filter these bad airs. "And thanks to our precautions of cleanliness, sobriety, and judicious ventilation, not one person here contracted the sickness. Where windows and doors are kept jealously shut, there cholera will find its easiest entrance. However, you must be sure to close your window again after dark. Disease of the miasma type is always more likely to be contracted in the evening."

I promised to take care. I had also to subject myself to a dosing with Eno's Fruit Salts. It was easier to accept the glass of sparkling laxative Mr. Bittern handed me than to argue whether the claims on the bottle's label were true. Purifying the blood was said to be an effective preventative against the malaria which was swimming side by side with the cholera.

Although fastidious on the tedious hygiene rules, Mr. Bittern was, overall, a different man from the one I had left behind. He seemed smaller.

Admittedly I had put on three full inches. But his entire physical stature had diminished. His shoulders drooped. His chest was now concave as though he no longer had the energy or the will to stand tall. His sandy-coloured hair had grown pale and scanty and was scraped halfheartedly across the top of his head. He looked as though he had scarcely eaten or slept all the time I had been away, though he may have wept much, for the flesh of his face appeared to have puffed out and sagged wearily off his cheekbones like that of a carp that has lain too long in the sun.

I was no longer afraid of him, but we were both of us still trapped into a relationship neither of us had wanted.

He was not a cruel man, but his rigidity of ideas made up for his lack of it in his posture.

He never beat me. He never let me starve for food. He continued to ensure that I was decently clothed and kept informed of the necessary precautions to take against fever and disease.

But he would not educate me. It was not the cost of a tutor that irked him.

"To educate you would be an inappropriate and nonsensical use of effort."

I was thirsting for an education, any education. The more I saw, the more I knew how inadequate I was in my ignorant state. Mary had increased my thirst.

"This thirst of which you speak," said Mr. Bittern, "is a phantom, a fanciful luxury of your mind. Every human endeavour in life must be for a purpose, directed to an end. The aim of education is to fit children for the position which they are thereafter to occupy. If you were a normal boy, who was going to go out into the world, you would attend school or have a tutor. But you are not a normal boy."

I dared to answer back. "And if I am not educated, how shall I gain a livelihood?"

"Your current position is ambiguous. Your future position even more so. You will never be able to work, to earn your own bread, to make your own way in life. You will always need to have a protector. You are well housed here. You have the gardens to walk in, but you must keep away from the ornamental pond."

It was another well-known fact of the bursar's that low-lying evening mists rising from lakes or ponds were especially sinister.

"Is that all I am to do with the rest of my life, walk between the herbaceous borders?"

As Mr. Bittern sank deeper into the grief of widowhood, I sank deeper into the stupor of boredom and ignorance. When my mother was alive, I had at least had those clandestine forays to Kew and Hammersmith. Now there was nothing, no prospects and no future.

My thoughts turned increasingly to the purpose of life or death. There seemed little purpose in either. Jack-Paolo had been a wise and prescient child, and the six hundred washed from the *Queen of the Thames* and obliged to swallow the poisoned waters were the fortunate few.

For hours I paced my room. I saw nobody and nobody knew I was there. At night I was unable to sleep, for my mind and my body had been so underused.

In spite of Mr. Bittern's dire warnings of the mortal and moral dangers of self-gratification, I found it impossible to exercise control in the way he wished. Besides, it seemed that self-control was not worth so very much since the seizures continued under any circumstances.

During one of the dark periods of black melancholy that followed a grand mal attack, I asked myself if this imprisonment was perhaps all of my own making.

There were no physical restraints, chains, padlocked gates, holding me. I was a hundredfold freer than many of my age, freer than Lawrie enslaved in perpetuity at Giddings's lodgings, freer than apprentices locked into seven years of unpaid service, freer than a condemned pickpocket with only expulsion to the far side of the world to free him, freer than the palsy boys whose limbs could never obey.

Since I already had my liberty, I resolved to use it to benefit myself. I would start with the familiar. Once, flower painting for profit had been the one brightness in an empty existence. I would resume painting, though now I would copy not from other flat pictures but from life.

I put on my cap and ventured out, down the gravel path, between the tidily planted fuchsia and clarkia and lupin of the herbaceous borders, over the rough grass, along the bank to the water meadows. Boldly I gathered the flowers growing wild, trefoil, cow parsley, swamp lily, water hawthorn, and carried them back to my room. After reviving them in the water jug on my washstand, I set to work and worked for a week.

The completed paintings were fine, competent renderings of riverside plants. I was proud of them. But I did not show them to Mr. Bittern. With his opinions and categorical assertions, he would certainly have firm views on flower painting and would doubtless condemn it as an unfit activity for any youth, even a useless and incapacitated one.

Over the next weeks, I searched out and set out paper examples of everything I could find, from the bog arum to the water plantain, from the dainty water hyacinth to the ugly, toadlike bur reed. And even when I had to wade knee-deep through a tangle of myrtle flags or slither along a willow branch overhanging the river, no harm came to me, either from fits and drowning or from the pestilent vapours rising from swampy pools.

Tentatively, I ventured further. Mr. Bittern was so enshrouded in his misery he did not notice. I reached the Public Reading Rooms, newly opened for the use of ordinary folk, in the village of Isleworth. Here, with the enthusiastic assistance of the librarian, who took me not for the mental degenerate that I was, but for a fellow amateur botanist, I was able to get a firm identification for each of my paintings.

Twice a day, the busy waterway flowed down to the sea. Twice a day, the tide flooded it back. Back and forth, taking with it sticks and leaves, eels and elvers, dead fish and dogs, living people, and all kinds of cargo. Once, it had taken me but I had been washed back up. Since leaving Margate, I had done nothing but wallow in self-pity and paint pretty flowers. I must become waterborne again. On impulse, I decided I would go to sea. I could go to sea.

In the Public Reading Rooms, I studied for my future as a seaman.

The librarian was sadly bemused by my abrupt change of interest from botany to navigation but nonetheless supplied me with the books I needed so that I could learn the means of fixing a ship's position by measuring, with a sextant, the angle of one of the heavenly bodies above the horizon at a given time.

I read the theory of the use of the compass, the chronometer, and the log. When the angle of the heavenly body above the horizon had been ascertained, the navigator must consult his Nautical Almanac, whose tables would show the position of the sun and the stars on every day at various hours in the forthcoming year. From the tables, the navigator calculated the geographical position from which the sun, or other heavenly body, would make such an angle above the horizon at that particular time.

By rote, I learned, wishing all the while that I could have had the brain of Jack-Paolo, Italian sailor's son, who could absorb the data of one thousand and one tabulae without needing even to think what he was doing.

I memorized the traditional hours of the watches. The chief officer's watch was from four o'clock in the morning until eight in the morning, and from four in the afternoon till eight in the evening. Second officer's watch was from midnight till four in the morning, and from midday till four in the afternoon. And third officer's watch was all the rest.

Although I could not become a Master, or even a lesser officer, I could become a noncommissioned rating and I saw myself as standby on the dog-watch. I must check the ship's course, take account of others in the vicinity and of rocks, icebergs, and other hazards. I must keep an eye on the weather, the barometric pressure, the likelihood of gales and sudden squalls. I must watch out for the load-line. The differing levels of salinity in the various seas around the world would cause the ship to rise or fall higher or lower in the water.

The rating must keep alert at all times. I must be too busy ever to bemoan my lot.

But watch-keeping, like poring over dry books, can become tedious. It is easy enough to fall asleep in midocean, or into a reverie, and not to see the approaching gale, the seventeen-foot waves towering up like walls, until too late.

A seizure came upon me without a warning. I came to on the wooden floor of the Reading Rooms, groggy and uncertain where or who I was. Nobody had seen me but the librarian, who picked me up.

"Drunks may not use this library," he said. "Please do not come again when you are intoxicated!"

The damning significance of the fall reached me. It was one thing to fall to the floor of a quiet rustic library and quite another to fall when on duty on the high seas while my trusting colleagues slept in their hammocks. Even if I did not tumble overboard into the savage swell, the lives of all would be endangered.

I closed the book on navigation and returned it to its shelf, knowing that I must not give up. I must fight passivity. Even if I could never master the dangers of water, there was another way out. I had been searching in the wrong place for my escape.

Twelve

⁓⁓⁓

I had the right to take any risks. It was my life to do what I would with, just as Mr. Bittern's was his own, and if he wished to let his be eaten away by perpetual grief, that was his risk and his choice.

Mine was going to be to live, to try to discover the world and everything in it.

I selected from the folder beneath my bed half a dozen of the best of my wildflower paintings. I mounted them carefully, as my mother used to do, placed them in a folder, and took them to Dukes and Sons, the Stationers and Printers of repute.

I got to see Mr. Dukes himself, as he had just come in from his luncheon. "You may remember, sir," I began uncertainly, "some time back, how you used to buy flower paintings to use for greeting cards?"

"Indeed I did."

"Well, I have brought some more new ones to show you."

He seemed disinterested. But I knew mine were good. So, rapidly, I pulled one from the folder to show him.

He looked at it, then spent some time inspecting the rest, in a good light, and under a magnifying glass.

"Yes, of course, I recognize the style, though these are different in temperament. We bought quite a number? Your mother, is it not?"

I nodded.

"They're very pretty, son. But I fear you must tell your mother there is not so much demand for this kind of rustic painting at the moment, nicely done though they may be. Fashion ebbs and flows on the whims of I know not what." He handed them back.

I replaced them slowly. I would have to find some other means of gaining the modest amount of money I required for a one-way ticket to where the real painters were.

"Well, send her my regards, son. Tell her 'exotica,' that's the fashion now. We've done with roses and violets and all that for the time being. What they want now is this foreign stuff. Poinsettia, hibiscus, heliconia. You know, plants and flowers, fruit even, from exotic climes. Madeira, Crete, Oleander, that's a lovely one, from Italy they say. And bird of paradise, that is a beauty, from Madeira. All the places they go. And even when the folks don't go travelling, they like to have these foreign things they've seen in the Botanical Gardens. So if she's got the time to do some exotica, I'd be more than happy to buy them."

"Could you please write the names for me," I asked. "So that I'll make no mistake in telling her."

He did so.

"And if my mother were to find pictures of these plants, and make copies, and I were to bring them to you, you would buy them from me?"

"Indeed I would!"

"If I have your word, then I shall find them," I said. "Definitely."

So I moved with growing excitement to a new form as an artist, as a meticulous copyist of plants whose like I had never before seen.

The librarian at the Public Reading Rooms, relieved that I had returned to a botanical interest, obtained the necessary volumes for me. These were not the fuchsia or lupin of an English herbaceous border, nor the delicate wild blooms from a tangled English waterside. Many of these peculiar plants came complete with diagrams of their roots systems, their pods, the insides of their fruits opened up, like the medical charts on the walls of a physician's consulting room. One of the books had been printed in Germany, and the labelling was in Latin and German, neither of which I could understand. So I merely copied the copperplate script as carefully as I could.

Among the plants were orchids and water chestnuts, tuberous plants with twisting tendrils and dark fleshy stems like human limbs, some even coloured the freckled or pinkish colours of human skin. There was one that even seemed to be carnivorous, taking flies from the air to sustain it. The only two I recognized were the pomegranate and the date-palm.

I prepared two dozen paintings, each of a different species. I mounted them and wrapped them carefully in the pillowcases from my bed, then in brown paper, as protection. With anxiety about whether I might be taken by a seizure on the way and so lose my work, or whether I might find that Mr. Dukes had changed his mind, I set out. All the way, my heart was pounding and my mind churning.

Mr. Dukes was out when I arrived. His assistant knew nothing of the purpose of my visit. So I sat on a wooden chair and waited with the parcel clasped on my knee. I still feared that a seizure might come and spoil my chances and my work, so I said to the assistant, "I will wait for Mr. Dukes, but should anything happen to me while I am waiting, please make sure that this parcel, which he is expecting, is lifted to a safe place."

The assistant had no idea what I meant.

I waited for two hours as customers came and went. At last Mr. Dukes himself returned and was surprised to see me. But, after inspecting my exotica, he was true to his word and bought every single one for half a guinea each.

"These are beautifully done. Your mother must have worked very hard," he said. "I think they will go well. Tell her I will take more of this kind if she will do them."

"No, that is not possible," I said. "My mother will not be able to paint any more like this, for she is going abroad."

I tucked the money into my sock so that, should I take a fit on the way back to the Academy, there was less risk that I might be robbed of it while unconscious.

Then I planned my departure.

Mr. Bittern put no impediment in my way.

"I have heard," he said, "that the Mediterranean climate, being warm and dry, is helpful to your condition."

He himself was tightly enshrouded in a lambswool shawl against the possibility of taking a chill from a draught.

He gave me ten guineas to augment the money I had received for the floral exotica, and he wrote a letter to his cousin who had been taking the waters in Vichy and now lived in a *pensione* in Ventimiglia.

"My cousin was never an easy person to get on with," he said. "But at least the *pensione* is said to be quiet and entirely satisfactory."

I wanted almost no luggage, just my mother's watercolours, a supply of cartridge papers, a sketch pad and pens, clean socks, three handkerchiefs, and, on Mr. Bittern's advice, a sun hat.

"Be cautious," he warned. "The Italian sun is rumoured to be treacherous. It is hotter than it seems and causes sunstroke and apoplexy. Keep indoors, but with the window open."

For the second time I travelled down the river which seemed both a friend and an enemy. The cook had prepared for me, as before, a pack of cold mutton sandwiches and pickle, though I was too apprehensive to eat. This time I sat not in the bows to watch where I was heading, but in the stern to watch what I was leaving behind, all my rotten childhood and its memories of oppression and defeat, to try to find something fresh under the perfidious foreign sun.

From the Pool of London, there was a daily sailing on the Batavia Line to Rotterdam, and I took it.

At the busy port of Rotterdam, my confidence almost failed me. Having disembarked, I had to find my way to the railway terminus. The stevedores working on the quayside spoke another language whose intonation seemed to be like my own. But they understood nothing of what I asked. Besides, they were busy unloading the ship and had no time to waste on one wandering youth in a Norfolk jacket and sun hat.

I so lost my nerve that I was tempted to reboard the ship on which I had just arrived. But then I tried asking an elderly porter and he, more helpfully, vigorously pointed out the direction I should take. Recalling my mother's advice on the importance of tipping, I gave him one of my foreign coins to recompense him for his trouble. He looked at it thoughtfully, bit upon it, then showed it to a companion. Perhaps it was not enough?

I offered him a second foreign coin but he refused to accept it.

The journey was to be a night and two days long. Once I had found the security of the correct train and my place on it, beside a window, I began to relax enough to nibble at the cold mutton, and even began to enjoy myself a little.

The train trundled through the flat Flemish lowlands, where everything was extraordinarily and exhilaratingly different from everything I previously knew. If the train had not been so shaky, and if I had not been so shy of people staring, I would have taken out my sketch pad there and then. It was like a continuous moving picture as meadows and villages, haystacks, hills, churches, were passed before my eyes. The fields were a different shape, the crops were different, the farm buildings were built in another style. The people working in the fields wore unfamiliar garments. Even the sky was different. When the train slid between the tall backs of the buildings of Paris, I had half exhausted myself with so much looking.

There was a wait of one hour at the station named Gare de l'Est before the train resumed its course south, too long a time to sit patiently, too short to wander the streets of Paris and search for the great galleries of classical art. So I merely walked the length of the platform several times over, breathing the air of Paris and with the exhaltation of travel saturating my being.

When I returned to my place, the carriage was filling. A couple travelling with two children came aboard, then an older woman, and then, moments before the train was due to leave, a late passenger, large and elderly, bald with a curly beard and loose ill-fitting clothes. He had a great deal of luggage, cases of all shapes and sizes as well as a hatbox, a folding wickerwork camp chair, and a pair of canvas saddle-bags. The other passengers all had to move up to make space while his porter stowed his things unsteadily on the overhead racks from where they were in no danger of toppling down the moment the train started forward.

When this cumbersome old fellow was finally settled, puffing and wheezing, he glared angrily round at the rest of us through gold-rimmed spectacles and declared, in English, "Paris! Paris! Never again. Remind me never, never to go there again! All the devils in hell are to be found in Paris and I have not slept a wink for two nights!"

I hoped that none of the others were English-speaking Parisians who might take offence at this outburst.

"Four hundred and seventy-three cats at least were all at once outside my hotel room making an infernal row, making sleep or work or even thought impossible. Next time I shall go to India, or Sardinia, or Jumbsibojigglequack, or anywhere but Paris!"

After ranting and complaining a good deal more, he finally settled to muttering to himself till the train attendant came down the corridor, ringing a little brass bell to summon those who were rich enough or foresighted enough to have booked sleeping apartments in another carriage. The old man fussed and fretted a good deal about whether his luggage would be safe to leave.

I had not anticipated that Italy was such a long way distant and that this journey would seem so very long. I passed the night upright in my seat in the corner of the compartment, sleeping only snatches. I dreamed a dreary dream of dark overhanging rocks and of a pale lonely figure trudging along beneath them, never managing to reach the end of the track before nightfall. Then the track turned to water and now he was rowing upstream against the tide beneath the menacing rocks, again still not managing to reach the end before nightfall.

When I woke, I was no longer elated with this journey of which there was still another day to go.

After they had breakfasted in the dining-car, the fat old man and the couple with their two small children resumed their seats.

The children had a book of pictures and verses from which the mother was reading aloud to help pass the time and prevent them from growing restless. At first, I did not listen, but then I recognized the verses as being the same ones as in the torn coverless book of Mary's, concerning deformed people to whom unfortunate things occurred.

The little girls giggled quietly, especially when their mother pointed out to them that the train would eventually be passing Aosta, the very place named in one of the verses.

The children's father struck up a conversation with the fat man.

"Do you know this book, sir?" he asked in a friendly manner.

The old man said that he did.

"Then you must know that thousands of families are grateful to the author for providing such delight and entertainment for their little ones."

The old man nodded in agreement.

"However, the identity of the author," the younger man said, "is not generally known to the public at large."

"Is that so?" said the old man.

"It is really Lord Derby who wrote these lines."

The old man interrupted. "But it is a Mr. Lear who wrote them. See on your children's book, it has the name printed. Edward Lear, both on the cover and upon the title-page." He seemed upset by the other man's suggestion that it was some lord who had written them. But then, as he had shown by his behaviour when he boarded the train at Paris, he was clearly a man easily irritated.

"Aha, yes," said the children's father. "That is because Edward, Earl of Derby, being a man of some breeding, chose not to publish his book openly under his own name, but under an anonym. If you transpose the letters of the assumed surname, Lear, you will find it reads, simply, Earl. Thus Edward, Earl, writer and illustrator of this excellent book."

The fat old man grew indignant, like a kettle about to boil over. He took out a spotted handkerchief to wipe his bald brow, which did look quite hot.

He said, "But I happen to know, intimately, the very person, Edward Lear. He is the renowned artist who has sold paintings to many members of the aristocracy and given lessons to her majesty the queen. He is also the author who wrote and illustrated the whole of this little book which is amusing your children!"

Whereupon the other replied, "And I have good reason to know, sir, that you are wholly mistaken. For there is no such person as Edward Lear."

It struck me as a foolish and entirely unnecessary argument. Both men seemed so sure of their facts that if one had not been in the company of his daughters and his wife, and if the other had not been a lame old man with shortsight, they might have got up and fought one another.

The old man protested, "But there *is* such a man. And I am that man! And I wrote that book!"

The younger man laughed in a mocking and condescending way, as if he took the old fellow to be a liar and quite mad. With difficulty, the old man stood up in the moving train, removed his hat and showed round the inner hatband, which was stamped with the name Edward Lear. Triumphantly, he showed also his handkerchief, which was similarly named.

The family, much subdued, offered many apologies, which the old man graciously accepted, and a truce was declared.

However, the little girls had grown restless and were squirming about like tadpoles, one on her mother's lap, the other on the seat. As though to prove that peace had been reached, the old man, now in an improved humour with his eyes twinkling behind his spectacles, offered to tell the children a story.

The elder of the girls nodded.

"Would you have a story of the Land of Gramblamble?" the old man asked the child seriously. "Or The Tale of the Lake Pipple-Popple and the Soffsky-Poffsky Trees, or The Story of a Plumpudding Flea?"

It was all such wordy nonsense that I felt the father would have been right to think the old fellow, if not a liar, at any rate entirely senile.

And the child was far too overawed to make any choice. So the old man just began anyway.

"Here beginneth a nonsense story of the four little children who went round the world. Their names were Violet, Slingsby, Guy, and Lionel, and they all thought they should like to see the world. So they bought a large boat to sail quite round the world by sea."

Owing to my sleepless night, I only half listened. But anyway, it was an entirely preposterous tale in which children climbed into a tea-kettle when tired, and where animals could speak.

I dozed on and off and the narrative continued. Or perhaps he had begun a new story.

As we approached the foothills of the mountains, the landscape became hillier, less verdant, more rock-strewn. We entered a tunnel of seemingly endless darkness where the sounds and movements of our train were distorted. Then we emerged, as suddenly as a toad leaping from its hole, into a markedly different landscape. Now we were running through a narrow mountain gorge, and the only view was of the wall of rock with small waterfalls bouncing down it and twisted lonely trees growing askew from cracks, and high above us on a precipitous ledge I saw a goat, precariously perched like a parrot on a branch, stretching out its bearded neck to reach a leaf on a straggly tree.

The old man's voice rose louder, sank softer, and was speaking so much nonsense of fruit trees that grew fishes and seas which were coloured purple.

I thought the goat would fall. And if it fell, it would fly through the air downwards to the track.

The sheer rock-face grew taller till it was blocking out the light and all the brightness of the sky, and the compartment grew dim. There was just a small jagged shape of light left high above us.

I felt my left hand grow tight. My arm began to tremble. There was nothing I could do.

The old man's voice went out and I could hear it clearly now.

"But the Blue Boss-Woss plunged into a perpendicular, spicular, orbicular, quadrangular, circular depth of soft mud, where in fact his house was."

The sky was falling in. The fearsome dark rock was going to overpower me.

I knew what was going to happen. And yet I did not know.

"And the seven young fishes, swimming with great and uncomfortable velocity, plunged also into the mud quite against their will, and not being accustomed to it, were all suffocated in a very short period."

Inside my head came an explosion like a million tons of dynamite. The pain was impossible.

After all, I did know what was happening and I was swept through with utter disappointment. I had hoped to leave all this behind, and yet here it was following me.

But this time was unlike any of the previous times. The pain was intense and the terror overwhelming. This time I knew that irreversible damage was being done to my brain and that I was going to die.

Thirteen

—⚬⚬⚬—

*T*he room had a raftered ceiling. I lay staring at it for a while. The walls were plain plaster, painted a glowing ochre, or perhaps it was the reflection of the golden light from outside. There was the sound of pigeons cooing and, distantly, of children playing.

If I was dead, this place was not hell, but nor was it heaven, for I had a severe headache, was confused and depressed. Perhaps it was the place limbo, neither heaven nor hell, to which, so Mary told me, Jack-Paolo had gone.

I crept warily across the red-tiled floor to the window and perceived that I could not be dead. On the outside were green wooden shutters, which I pushed open. The villa was set in a grove of olives, with slopes to either side speared with the tall cypress trees. The air was soft and dry. Directly ahead was a clear view of the water of the Mediterranean, not narrow and sullen as on the Thames, nor grey and turbulent as on the English Channel, but as wide and lucid and gently blue as the sky above it. And I felt that this must surely be the pure and beneficial water for which I had been searching all my life.

I returned to bed and slept.

When I woke, some books and an English newspaper had appeared at the bedside.

A dark-complexioned man who spoke in a language I could not understand brought me, at intervals, water, tea, and soup, which I was too nauseous to take. Understanding this, he brought me a wineglass full of sweet aromatic liquid.

"Marsala, Marsala," he said, indicating that this was the name of the wine in the glass, and I should drink it.

It smelled like cough mixture though did indeed perform wonders at restoring my appetite so that when he brought me a dish of more sustaining food, though of a type I did not recognize, I was able to eat.

I asked, "Where am I? What is this place? Where are my clothes? Where is my luggage, my wallet, my travel papers?"

The manservant shrugged, not understanding a word, and left. But he returned with a gentleman's green silk dressing-gown and showed me down to a terrace, with chairs and a table beneath a canopy of vines.

The villa appeared to be the home of a painter, for the passages and rooms through which I had been led were stacked with landscape paintings and watercolours, in finished and unfinished condition, framed and unframed.

Set out upon the table was my sketchbook and my mother's watercolour palette. My sable brushes had been carefully placed upright in a jar. The manservant indicated by more hand gestures and rapid speaking in his own tongue that my captor, or host, whichever it was, was busy elsewhere in the building and not to be disturbed.

The terrace was a profusion of full-blown roses with little white cluster flowers in between. Beyond it was a luxuriant garden overflowing with an abundance of tropical vegetation.

Since there was no way I could leave wearing only an outsized dressing-gown, I resigned myself to making some use of my captivity in this charming prison. I was of two minds over whether to attempt to catch the distinctive dark features of the manservant, who was at the far end of the terrace keeping his eye on me while simultaneously shelling peas into a basin, or the variegated beauty of the spiky shrubs and floral abundance ahead.

Overawed by the dark man's constant vigilance, I decided on the view from the terrace. But when I opened my sketchbook, I found someone had been trespassing there.

Alongside one of the rough sketches I had made for the floral exotica for Dukes Printers was a pen drawing of another kind of flower. At first glance, it looked like a robust Dutch tulip. On a closer inspection, the bloom growing from the top of the stem was a wooden washtub and the stamens of the flower were pixie faces peering out.

Underneath was written *Washtubbia Pixicalis*, and I guessed the identity of the trespasser. It was the plump old man who had told silly stories on the train.

All afternoon, I sat on his terrace dabbling with my watercolours or dozing to the sounds of the fluttering pigeons and the buzzing insects.

In late afternoon, the old man emerged from his studio in his baggy clothes with his bushy beard as luxuriant as his flower beds.

He sat down heavily on a chair beside me and the manservant immediately brought him a glass full of the thick brown Marsala drink.

With a sigh he said, "No bird is more beautiful than a pigeon."

I feared he was going to tell me a long and foolish children's story and quickly gathered up my possessions from the table.

From the argument on the train with the other passenger, I knew his name to be Lear.

"Mr. Lear, sir, I believe I should thank you for helping me in whatever way you did when I was indisposed. And now, just as soon as I have my clothes returned, I will be on my way and bother you no longer."

"My dear child," he said, "I regret that you cannot leave yet. I have spoken to the doctor about your condition, and he advises that you should have a baked barometer for your breakfast and two thermometers stewed in treacle for supper. And since keeping an empty stomach is always hazardous, I suggest that as soon as you are hungry as a pumpkin pie, we should both sit down to a splendidophorospherostiphongious dinner prepared for us by Giorgio. I have been grinding my nose to a standstill in my studio and certainly need a chubbly celebration."

I demanded firmly, "Why did you bring me here?"

"Because of all creatures, children are the most interesting and I am a respectable old cove who is fond of children. You must not bother yourself about my scabbiousnesses."

"I am not a child," I said stiffly.

"And nor am I, alas, though often I wish I were an egg about to hatch."

"Why did you take pity on me?"

"Because most human beings are awful idiots, barring a few exceptions, of which you are clearly one. Your sweetly susceptible name I have deduced to be Edward. My home is *Villa Eduardo*, which is Italian for *Edward's House*, so it would appear that this house has been constructed expressly for you. And since I know who you are, do you know who I might be?"

I did not say that I knew him, from our first encounter, to be a grumpy old man. Instead, cautiously, I said, "I know that you are someone who does not like people who are rude."

"I do not care one nine hundred and ninety-ninth part of a spider's nose what anybody thinks of me, except my cat, whose opinions I hold in the highest esteem."

"And that you are also an artist who is at least well-known and maybe even very famous."

He shook his head slowly. "No, woefully wrong. I am Lord High Bosh and Nonsense Producer, also known as the Old Derry Down Derry, who loves to see little folks merry, and I would like us to be friends."

I said, "So I am to stay here and call you Mr. Derry?"

"Or you may call me Duncle because I would like to be your Adopty Duncle. You will find I am three parts crazy and wholly affectionate."

Duncle seemed a curious name till I understood the word-play. Almost everything he said had some mixed-up other meaning.

I wondered if I should be alarmed by this ancient fellow's interest. I wondered what he wanted from me.

I decided he was peculiar but probably harmless.

"Since you, too, are an honourable artist," he said, rising stiffly from his chair, "may I show you round my chumblious garnering?"

Since my head was still a little painful, I accepted to stay another night as his guest and to walk round his garden with him.

He was evidently immensely proud of it. He shuffled breathlessly along the paths. Summer flowers were spilling everywhere in a giddy abundance.

I followed, holding up the trailing sides of the dressing-gown. A cat with no tail came after us, managing to get under his feet at every step. When he stopped to point out to me some particularly luxuriant flower, the cat twisted itself like a clematis around his ankles. He spoke of each of the plants as though they were his much-loved grandchildren.

After our dinner, Mr. Lear sat on the terrace with his tailless cat purring upon his lap and a Greek Testament in his hand. As the sun went down, the heavy scent of the numerous flowers filled the air.

He did not seem to be in a mood to speak. He was watching the darkening sea. Sitting so still with the cat on his lap, and his high domed head and abundant curling beard, he made an interesting model. So I sketched his likeness in my book.

At length he said, "It is very much like paradise here, but Adam hath no Eve."

I took him to mean that, having no wife, he was lonely and I supposed that this was the real reason he had brought me to his house.

I said, "Did you capture me to keep you company?"

He said, "I have not kidnapped or goatnapped you, or mousenapped. I had you brought here because I saw you suffering alone from one of the most distressing and intolerable conditions to which humans are subject. It is scarcely possible to conceive an object more loudly calling for a bystander's compassion than witnessing a child with your melancholy condition."

"Why did you not leave me to the care of the train attendant?"

"The vile beastly rottenheaded footbegotten pernicious priggish screaming tearing roaring perplexing splitmercrackle insane ass of an attendant, not to mention the priggish mentally-decomposed physician he called, nor to mention the other ill-conducted caterwauling passengers, had not the least notion how to care for you. And most were for throwing you off the train and into a deep ravine."

He was so distressed that I wished I had not brought up the subject of my seizure.

When my clothes were returned to me by Giorgio, the shirt washed and ironed, the jacket pressed, it seemed I was free to leave. But now I wanted to stay at least another day, for Mr. Lear was going out on a sketching outing the following morning and had said that I could accompany him if I wished.

We set out early when the light was still rosy. Mr. Lear rode on a donkey with his ungainly legs dangling down each side, and the manservant followed behind laden with lunch and drawing materials. I wore my sun hat and carried my sketchbook.

When we came to a possible subject, Mr. Lear dismounted, took his drawing block from Giorgio, lifted off his spectacles, and gazed for several minutes silently at the scene through a monocular glass. Then he laid down the glass on a rock, readjusted his spectacles, and put to paper the exact view before us with its mountain range, the distant glimpse of bluebell sea, the tiny hilltop village, the twisty trees in the foreground, with a rapidity and accuracy that inspired me to try to do the same.

We continued in this way till he had completed half a dozen landscapes. After each stop, he asked if he might see my work, too, and always offered encouragement with the gentlest of advice so that, in a single day, I felt I had discovered more about technique than I had discovered in my whole previous life.

It was a peaceful yet exciting day.

Quite unexpectedly, Mr. Lear asked Giorgio to pack up his things, and we returned in a rush so that the poor donkey had to trot most of the way with the plump rider on its back.

When we reached the villa, Mr. Lear seemed in a strange agitated mood, as though anxious to get something done. Without speaking, he went straight up to his room.

I sat alone on the terrace eating my minestrone and roast chicken and marvelling at the beauty of the night, of the view with the lights twinkling from the houses on the sea's edge. I felt in a kind of ecstasy over the visual excitements I had seen and the pleasure of being out in the sun and open spaces all day. I was startled by sounds of some commotion from Mr. Lear's room.

I supposed the manservant would respond. The commotion continued, and then the crash of furniture falling and breaking glass. It sounded like men fighting. I feared it might be thieves after Mr. Lear's more valuable paintings. Giorgio was evidently not on the premises. I ran indoors. The noise was coming from Mr. Lear's bedroom, so I ran upstairs.

His door was closed and there was no response when I

knocked. Privacy, he had told me, was very important to him. I hesitated, then, risking his annoyance, I opened his door.

I was astonished by what I found.

Mr. Lear was upon his bed, his big ungainly body thrashing and juddering with the spasms of a vigorous convulsion. His spectacles lay on the floor with a cracked lens. The lamp was smashed, the beside table lying on its side.

So he, too, was a victim of the dark sickness.

Knowing from experience how it is with a seizure, I stayed with him till it was over. I set the room to rights, and when he came back to the world, I reassured him who he was and where he had been, and helped him out of his cumbersome outer garments, and into his night-shirt. I offered to fetch him a drink, which he declined, and I sat with him till he fell into a natural sleep.

I felt overcome by admiration and affection for him. I knew I had discovered at last my true kinsman. I would, after all, ask if I might stay there. I had been forced to live with a stepfather not of my choosing. Now I was selecting my own adopted uncle.

Giorgio returned soon after, and very drunk.

If I had surmised that it was Mr. Lear's wish to keep me there, I discovered next morning how entirely wrong I was.

After my own breakfast, I went to find him. He was not at work in his studio but lying on a sofa with his cat. Despite his size, he looked so frail that he might blow away on a breath of wind. He regarded me suspiciously. He had perhaps been only half aware of my presence the previous night.

I explained that I had been there with him but had done no more than he must have done for me on the train.

"Aha, yes, a return of the old affliction in the head," he said. "It appears it has shaken off one of my toes, two teeth, and three of my whiskers. But mercifully it has passed. Was Giorgio about?"

I explained how Giorgio had not returned till past midnight and that since I spoke no Italian I had said nothing to him.

"It is wonderful that these fits of mine have never been discovered, for, apprehending them beforehand, I go to my room. You must learn to do the same."

I said that I usually managed to, but was sometimes caught out.

"All my life," said Mr. Lear, "I have managed to keep this a private matter. These things are not spoken of. This affliction has never, till now, been discovered by any other except the sister who cared for me, and she has taken the knowledge with her to the grave."

I said, "Then we each have our secrets. But it is no secret that I would like to accept your generosity and live here and learn to become an artist."

"I am often a miserable curmudgeon, and I must confess that since your arrival, I have felt cheerier and weller than for a long while. Your youth has brought back the calm and brightness of the view, the lovely sweetness of the air, the infinite days and years of outdoor delight. I am thankful for the temporary blessing of your presence. But you cannot stay."

"But, Mr. Lear, here in your garden, for the first time in my miserable life I have found true contentment."

"Contentment is a loathsome slimy humbug, fit only for potatoes, very fat hogs, and fools generally. Let us pray fervently that you may never become such an ass as to remain contented. You could indeed stay here and silently subsist on parrot pudding and lizard lozenges in chubbly content. But it would do you no good."

I pleaded, and eventually, through sheer exhaustion, he said I might stay till the end of the month.

"But then you must go. Even if you were content to eat nothing but little figs in summertime and worms in winter as I do, I cannot let you stay longer."

"I can be the best companion you ever had. I understand your situation like no one else. I will be quiet. I will clean your brushes, stretch your canvasses."

"You, Edward, are just beginning the battle of life. I am near the end of mine. I am walking already in the dusty twilight of the incomprehensible. You are newly hatched. And one thing is certain for someone of your special disposition. You must keep moving. A sedentary life will finish you off most suddenly. Although you will find that travel and change is full of heaps of botherations, it will affect you for better rather than worse."

This was a different wisdom from all that I had hitherto received. Always I had been advised to keep cloistered and still.

"But what, Mr. Lear, am I to make of my life when I have no education?"

"You can count yourself among the most blessed of cockfighters. Just suppose you had a complete education from one of the Bridges?"

"Bridges, Mr. Lear?"

"Bridge cities of learning. Oxbridge or Cambridge Universities, where the wise men are so foolish. Suppose you had been there, you would find yourself thrown out at the end of your matriculation and forced to become a teacher or a priest. And you would know exactly what lay ahead of you for the ensuing fifty years."

"But you were educated."

"I received none, beyond what my sister could teach me and what I learned with my eyes, which are now, alas, one hundred and two per cent failing me. I began to earn my living at fifteen and I am always thanking God that I never was educated, for it seems to me that nine hundred and ninety-nine out of every thousand of those who are so expensively and laboriously so, have lost all before they arrive at any decent age and remain cut and dry for life."

Giorgio came in with a glass of watered Marsala for his master.

"You, Edward, are in a world where there is far more good and pleasure than you can use up even in the longest life, provided you look for it. If you are to be a painter of any worth, which I have no doubt you will, you must see the world. For sheer beauty and wonder of foliage, you must go to Bombay. In a sieve you must go to sea."

"Bombay?" What a strange-sounding place. Was this one of his nonsense lands?

"It is in India."

I had, at least, heard of India.

"And there you will find oh, what new palms! And oh, what flowers! Oh, such creatures! Oh, such beasts! Anything more overpoweringly amazing cannot be conceived. Colours and costumes and myriadism of impossible picturesqueness.

And if, on your travels, people laugh at you, deflect their ridicule by being ridiculous. Do not allow the dark spirit to shadow your talent. You may not conquer it, but you must not let it conquer you."

He sighed and rested his head.

I had worn him out, just as I had said I would not.

"Yes," Mr. Lear agreed, "I am now feeling a little rusty-mustyfustydustybustycrusty."

So I left him to rest.

I went down to the terrace and applied the finishing touches to my watercolour impression of his abundantly flowered terrace. I signed, *For Dopty Duncle, from his most obedient nephew, Eduardo,* and placed it on the easel in his studio.

Then I fetched my bag, placed my sun hat upon my head, and set out to find my way to Bombay. As I strode down the track towards the bright sea I did not look back.

Endnote

———⚬∞⚬———

Misconceptions about epilepsy began in ancient times, when people believed that epileptics were possessed by demons and could only be cured by having the evil spirits cast out of their bodies. The loss of bodily control during an epileptic seizure was as terrifying to people then as it is today.

Today, however, we know that epilepsy is not madness or demonic possession, but a brain condition caused by a sudden change in how brain cells transmit electrical signals. There are more than twenty types of seizure syndromes, ranging from mild "blanking out" spells to heavy convulsions. Although in many cases there is no direct cause for the disease, epilepsy can be hereditary, or triggered by a head injury, brain tumor, drug use, or infection, and can develop at any time in life. The affliction affects two million Americans. Epileptics now can almost completely control their seizures with medication.

Edward Lear (1812–1888) was severely affected by epilepsy during a time in which antiepileptic drugs were unavailable, and the disease itself was misunderstood by most people. Lear suffered greatly from depression, asthma, and bronchitis as a child, as well as from the shame of his seizures. As an adult, he became so adept at predicting the seizures and hiding his disease that few people knew he had epilepsy.

Although in his time he was well known as a landscape painter, he is now remembered chiefly for his limericks and nonsense verse. He was a funny and highly creative man, who loved jokes and making up ridiculous expressions. In this story, almost everything Edward Lear says, including the silly made-up words, is based on his real sayings or writings. Some of the thoughts, fears, and experiences of the narrator, Albert Edward, are also based on the life and writings of Edward Lear.

—R. A.